SHADOW'S HOSTAGE

SHADOW ISLAND SERIES: BOOK SIX

MARY STONE
LORI RHODES

Copyright © 2023 by Mary Stone

All rights reserved.

No part of this book may be reproduced in any form or by any electronic or mechanical means, including information storage and retrieval systems, without written permission from the author, except for the use of brief quotations in a book review.

Created with Vellum

DESCRIPTION

When you're a hostage of your own nightmare…

As the Shadow Island Historical Society prepares to raise funds to restore the island's beloved lighthouse, someone else has other lethal plans. Instead of the presentation the group hopes for, they attract the attention of a madman claiming the historic monument is his family legacy before firing several shots and barricading the doors.

Now, one hostage is dying and the rest fear for their lives.

Interim Sheriff Rebecca West is no hostage negotiator, but she'll do whatever it takes to ensure the elderly captives are safely released. Especially when the perp turns out to be a local boy recently released from the mental hospital where he'd been committed since his mother abandoned him and his father. By all accounts, he's disturbed but harmless.

Or is he?

He's making outlandish assertions about the disappearance of his mother that don't make sense. And identifying missing persons who disappeared miles away. Are these accusations merely the delusions of mentally unstable man? Or is something more nefarious going on?

From its shocking beginning to the jaw-dropping conclusion, *Shadow's Hostage*—the sixth book in the Shadow Island Series by Mary Stone and Lori Rhodes—will make you realize we all see what we want to see, even if it's not true.

1

Eleanor Weever glanced back down for the hundredth time at the brochure she was reading.

"Nora, get your nose out of your reading. It's almost time."

She snapped her head up and blinked owlishly at her blurry best friend before remembering she needed to lower her chin to see over her new bifocals. "What?"

Gracie William wagged a bony finger. "I said it's almost time."

Already?

Nora still didn't believe the write-up in the brochure did the lighthouse justice, despite all the edits she'd insisted on to add more information. And Gracie didn't understand.

She closed the pamphlet and traced a finger down the cool wall of the structure, not liking how badly her age-spotted hand was trembling. She supposed it was just an indication of how much today mattered to her.

Everything needed to be perfect.

Noble Lighthouse was special. It hadn't been set on top of a hill to maximize its ability to warn sailors of danger.

Instead, the fifty-foot structure had been placed in its current location out of good old-fashioned spite.

Over a century ago, before Shadow Island became populous, the residents of a small cottage on prime real estate had refused to sell. That had pissed the other island folk right off. When a ship crashed off the shore, island officials used the accident to get their revenge on the cottage's owner by placing the lighthouse directly between their home and the ocean.

The tallest structure on the island rose from a ring of bald cypress trees, which had also been added to obstruct the neighboring cottage's view of the Atlantic. Both buildings were now landmarks with histories and lore embedded in the island's appeal. And if Nora could get her way, they'd soon become federally protected monuments.

She flipped a page in the brochure, smiling down at the image her own son had taken.

Unlike most others, this lighthouse was octagonal. Built near the mid-1800s, the framework was still solid despite the centuries of maritime abuse. Nora had worried herself sick that Hurricane Boris was going to topple the ancient structure. In the end, it remained.

Most of it anyway.

Even before the hurricane had come through, the lighthouse needed much repair. She looked up as far as the arthritis in her neck would allow. The blue July sky looked back.

Well, at least it isn't raining.

Gracie took the brochure out of Nora's hand and placed it on the stack of others. "Does the table look okay?"

Nora took off her bifocals, letting them hang from their beaded chain, and examined the array of finger foods Gracie had put together. Cheese and crackers were nestled next to bites of pepperoni and ham. Grapes and strawberries provided pops of color.

"It's perfect."

Gracie clasped her hands together. "I think it's the best cootie board I've ever made."

Nora giggled. Gracie couldn't say "charcuterie," and her substitute for the word tickled her every time.

"What about drinks?"

"I've got an array of juices and," Gracie lifted a large bowl, "I'm going to fill this with ice and little bottles of water."

Nora hugged her friend. "You've always been the perfect hostess."

Gracie pecked Nora on the cheek. "And you've always been the perfect bullshitter."

Nora didn't take offense because it was true.

She was the president of the Shadow Island Preservation Society, promoting today's event. If they had any hope of restoring the lighthouse to its former glory and turning it into the tourist attraction she knew it could be, she had to impress these people.

She just hoped her bullshitting was extra shitty today. There was so much resting on her ability to be persuasive and knowledgeable. The presentation had to go perfectly.

Picking up a lantern she wanted to use for the centerpiece, Nora shuffled back to the table and set it down. "Did you know the first lamps were from burning oil? And they used whale oil and other animal fats to fuel them? They…" Nora cut her oration short, lifted a hand to her chest, and inhaled as deeply as she could.

Gracie narrowed her eyes. "I told you to bring your oxygen with you, you old bat."

Nora sputtered a laugh. "It makes me look old."

Gracie snorted. "You *are* old." She traced her hand up and

down the center of her chest, breathing with the movement. "In…out." She repeated the orders until Nora felt better.

"I'm fine."

Gracie rolled her eyes. "Stick to the script we wrote. Remember, we're here to describe to the fundraising board how amazing this place will look in the future, not the past. They need to agree to release that money for the repairs."

Nora knew her friend was right, but truth be told, at eighty-one, she had many more years behind her than she did before her. It was sometimes hard to see too far ahead.

"I know. I know. I just…well, whale oil is obviously not something we'd use anymore and some of the committee members might find it interesting."

Gracie waved her off. "Go practice your speech. Bob and Chuck will be here soon. They promised to be here by ten thirty to help with last-minute things."

Doing as she was told, Nora wandered over to the entrance, imagining what she'd say after the full committee was here in—she glanced at her watch—a half hour. She already knew many of the committee members. She'd been privately trying to get them on board with her society's plans to bring the history of their island back into public knowledge.

Especially now.

With all the recent crime and death in her community, Gracie just wanted folks to focus on the more positive elements of the island and see the future that she envisioned.

"Welcome, everyone." She held out a hand, pretending to shake with an imaginary committee member. "Please take a look around so you can see for yourself what we've been telling you. As the lighthouse has aged, the structure has remained solid, but the interior landings and stairs, which were made primarily of wood, have fallen apart. Contrary to what that nasty reporter wrote, the lighthouse is decidedly *not* on the brink of collapse."

Bob Dolan appeared at the door. "Well, thank you, Nora."

Nora jumped and might've wet herself a little. She placed a hand over her racing heart. "You scared me, you devil."

Bob apologized but didn't look the least bit sorry as he stepped inside. "I was dared to climb to the top several times when I was a kid but never made it higher than the second turn. Everything past that was just too rickety."

Chuck Anderson came in behind him. "I did the same thing, which might be what's driven my desire to see this wonderful monument restored. So that one day we can safely walk all the way to the top of the lighthouse and see the view that enticed us all as children. That's why we're all here today."

Nora blew out a breath that felt too heavy in her lungs. "As I was attempting to say, before Bob nearly scared me into my grave," she shot him a baleful look, "I'm planning to have each committee member take a moment to inspect the walls as they enter. You can see the pitting that's started there. Don't let this molting fool you. The base is made of cut stone, while the tower is made of brick. Both sides are faced with stucco. It's only the outer skin that's crumbling, not the stone or brick."

She frowned as a person she didn't recognize stepped into the lighthouse. He was young, baby-faced, barely a man. He almost looked familiar with his shaggy brown hair, but she couldn't place him.

Was he a tourist who'd wandered in? He certainly wasn't on the fundraising committee.

Nora took a step toward the young man, prepared to tell him to leave. She stopped after noticing how he stared at everything with open wonder and joy.

That. Every person who comes to this island should be allowed to go inside this structure so they can feel exactly that way.

A young man interested in helping to preserve their city's heritage wasn't someone she wanted to shoo off. They needed to engage people of all ages. She hoped it looked rustic instead of run-down. She and the others had worked hard to clear out as much debris as they could, but there were still piles of wood along the walls mixed with the boxes of swag they'd paid to have made.

The merchandise included bells, thimbles, spoons, decorative plates, mugs, and even hoodies and ballcaps for the younger crowd. All the knickknacks tourists could possibly want. And all of them were decorated with the artist's version of what the lighthouse would look like once repairs were made.

Nora had spent so long working with a committee member's grandson using one of those flashy programs on that design. It was rewarding just seeing the image on something other than the young man's computer screen.

They were supposed to have had the samples up and on display already. But that hadn't worked with the days they'd lost to the storm. Now she was hoping an unpacking party would be enough.

As the young man stared up at the open sky, she resumed her speech.

"Now imagine this place once the changes are made. Couples on day trips, camping enthusiasts, and RVers can enjoy the views and amenities we've planned for our newly renovated Shadow Lore Lighthouse and gift shop!"

Shaggy stepped forward. "What did you say?"

"Oh, I'm sorry. I was rehearsing a speech I need to give a bit later on." Nora coughed into her hand and dabbed at the corner of her mouth with her linen handkerchief. "Today, we'll be talking about the exciting updates planned for this amazing lighthouse. We're rebranding the structure to reflect its new function and purpose. We even have mugs and t-shirts printed with the new name and likeness, Shadow Lore Lighthouse." Nora gestured toward the samples on display. "Are you someone's grandch—"

"No!"

The cry snapped Nora out of her rehearsed talking points and made her jump. "What?"

"It's the *Noble* Lighthouse!"

Nora gaped at the young man, who was no longer staring dreamily at the sky through the damaged top of the tower. He glared at her with a fury she'd never before experienced. He reached into his pocket and pulled out a black object, pointing it at her.

"What do you think you're doing?" Bob lunged at Shaggy, grabbing for his arm. A second later, they were tussling.

Chuck shuffled over, raising his cane over his head in what looked like slow motion.

Nora couldn't do much more than stare in horror as the fight raged on. It all ended with a loud bang. When a second shot rang out, Bob staggered back and threw his hands into the air in surrender. Chuck's cane fell to his feet.

"Nora!"

Gracie's hand wrapped around Nora's arm, pulling her back.

"Get back," Shaggy yelled, the gun pointing every which way.

Why's everyone yelling?

Nora gazed in confusion at the wild, angry brown eyes directed at her.

"You can't change the name! You'll ruin it!"

A third explosion followed his demands, and Nora fell backward. She hit the ground hard, and pain flared up her back and settled in her arm.

A burning, stinging throb nearly took her breath away, and she looked down. Blood pooled out from between her fingers, and she stared in horror as it soaked into her sleeve. Her arm didn't move when she attempted to lift it.

Nora tried to get to her feet with no luck. She didn't want the others to see her in such an undignified position, but she also had to get through to Shaggy. "Now, young man, calm down. We're here to help."

"You're in shock, Nora. He's got a gun!" Gracie screamed and tried to drag her dear friend away, pulling at her good arm while frantically keeping her eye on the crazed, gun-wielding man.

Nora looked around. Everything that had just happened snapped into place in her mind, and she realized what was going on. She'd been shot!

She tried again to get up as Gracie kept pulling at her. Her legs trembled, and her feet slipped, but Gracie wouldn't let go as she scooted backward, increasing the distance between them and the shooter. At least she was wearing trousers today and didn't have to worry about anyone seeing her underthings.

Shaggy whirled around, wildly waving the weapon at the cowering group. "I know what you're all really up to. I won't let you get away with this!"

Gracie stopped pulling, and Nora collapsed in a heap.

"Nora, your arm. Oh, God. Someone, call for help!"

Shaggy stomped closer, the barrel of the gun growing as big as the world. "No one is calling anyone or going anywhere! You'll stay right here. No one will ever destroy my family's leg-a-see. I won't let you!" He picked up one of the mugs and threw it. The ceramic burst into a thousand pieces.

"I don't understand." Nora's voice came out wispy. She tried to clear her throat but couldn't catch her breath. "The tour is just beginning. We want everyone to see…"

See what? She couldn't remember.

"Leave her alone!" It was Chuck.

Shaggy threw another souvenir mug, and Chuck barely ducked in time to avoid the missile. It exploded against the crumbling stucco.

Gracie screamed, and Nora looked up at her, terrified she'd been hurt. Gracie was staring across the room and Nora followed her line of sight. There was something wrong with her eyes. It shouldn't be so dark in the lighthouse. It was late morning, and the overhead sunlight poured down from the opening above them, where the keeper's hatch stood in disrepair.

Whatever happened that scared Gracie so badly was on the other side of the room. Nora tried to stand, but her legs were too weak.

"I'll leave her alone when she leaves my lighthouse alone. This is *my* lighthouse. My only home. My family leg-a-see!" Shaggy slammed the door closed and lowered the plank that locked the world outside. "You can't take it from me. It's all I have left of my mom!"

He spun around, shaking his gun at Nora again, and she looked into the dark tunnel that would deliver her death. Or maybe it already had.

"Your family?" Nora gasped. That couldn't be right. "This lighthouse was built by the Pickworths in 1832. They were paid by the Shadow Island township fund to protect the ships that would dock or pass by on their way to the mainland. Are you one of the Pickworths? I thought they'd all moved to the mainland by 1940. You're entirely too young to be one of them."

The young man gaped at her. "No, I'm not a Pickworth. I'm a Noble."

Chills ran through Nora, even though she felt so warm. It was silly to shiver like this in July. "Oh, like the last keeper of the lighthouse. This grand building was named after him in honor of his lifetime of service."

"Nora." Gracie yanked on her left arm, the one that hadn't been shot. "Now is not the time to go on one of your rambles."

Her head spinning, Nora looked away from the silhouette of the nice, young Noble boy and at her best friend. Gracie was fading.

Nora reached for her friend's face. "Don't go."

"Help, please," Gracie cried. "She's dying. We have to call 911."

Nora closed her eyes.

Oh, dear. That wouldn't do. They couldn't have someone die at the lighthouse. It would make it so hard to get the insurance they needed to turn this delightful landmark into a true tourist attraction.

2

Sheriff Rebecca West chugged down the last dregs of coffee as her senior deputy pulled his cruiser into a gravel driveway that was half weeds and all deep ruts. She longed to be back in her little sheriff's department, finishing up the remaining paperwork from their last big case.

She was exhausted from the events following a double homicide, as well as from the constant cleanup still needed after a hurricane plowed over the island. A few extra days to recuperate and get some additional sleep would be a godsend.

Is that too much to ask?

Apparently, it was.

"Didn't you say the call was for the old Alton Place?" Rebecca leaned forward, examining the construction site. The sign at the front declared it the future site of *The View at Shadow Inlet*.

"Yeah, this *is* the old Alton Place. They tore it down to build this new…whatever the hell it's supposed to be."

Hoyt Frost waved his hand at the driveway flanked by six partially built cottages and an army of construction workers on various tiers of scaffolding, literally throwing up brickwork faster than she thought possible. Two men in different colored hard hats noticed their arrival and walked over from where they'd been standing near a cement mixer.

"Nothing here looks old anymore," Rebecca muttered under her breath as she got out of the passenger seat.

It was a shame too. Back when she was a child, Rebecca's parents brought her to Shadow Island each summer. She remembered the houses being few and far between.

Now? Eager for a glimpse of the Atlantic Ocean, houses and condominiums were practically stacked on top of each other with yards no bigger than postage stamps.

"Sheriff?" The man in the white hat stuck his hand out to Hoyt.

The senior deputy pointed at her. "Sheriff Rebecca West."

The hand shifted her way, and he gave Rebecca's a solid shake. "I'm Stan Folton, in charge of this construction site. My foreman, LeRoy Bloom," he hiked his thumb over his shoulder at the man in the blue hat, "called me right after he called you guys. Said he had a man show up ranting and raving about us destroying his house."

"You weren't here during the incident?"

"No, ma'am. I just arrived a few minutes ago. I didn't want my guys getting harassed while trying to do their jobs. I brought the permits and a copy of our contract with the owners of this property. We didn't do the demolition. It was a scraped lot when we got started."

Rebecca turned her attention to Bloom. "Did you see the man?"

He squinted at her in the late morning sunshine, his blue hard hat doing little to keep the light out of his brown eyes. "Yes, ma'am. I heard him ranting as he walked up the road here. Then he started screaming."

Folton tried to hand her his clipboard of paperwork, and

she waved it over to Hoyt to look through. It would be incredibly unusual if they were, in fact, working on the wrong site. Right now, she wanted to focus on what happened.

"Could you hear what he was saying?"

Bloom laughed. "Oh, yeah. I heard him just fine. He walked right up the middle of the construction, acted like he was opening a door, then stood there staring and screaming about everything being out of place."

"Out of place?" She looked around at the mess of building materials. "What could he possibly think was out of place here?"

"The couch. Grandpa's chair. Ma's painting." Bloom waved his arms, as if pointing at different things around him. "Said the carpet was all covered in dirt too. Said he'd been robbed. That the trees took everything from him."

"Hold up." Hoyt moved several paces away, frowned, and looked around. He focused on the road and a few bald cypress trees still standing where the original driveway had been. Then he shifted a couple feet to the right and turned to face them. "Was he standing here?"

"Yeah, right about there. Then he walked off thataway," he pointed to Hoyt's left, "and started screaming that his bed was gone and that his dad had promised he'd always be welcome home once he got out."

How strange.

Hoyt tapped his foot on the ground, marking a spot. "This is where the Alton house was. Right over there, that's where Mason's childhood bedroom was. We got called out here often enough before he got committed."

"Committed?" Stan Folton straightened, his focus settled firmly on Hoyt, all amusement draining from his face. "Why was he committed? Are my men in danger?"

"Not sure what the diagnosis was. I know he was never

on great terms with reality, but he was never really violent either." Hoyt readjusted his hat lower on his forehead. "He'd throw temper tantrums and get loud. Act like he was hurt when he clearly wasn't. We were called out for disturbing the peace. And to double-check that he was okay, since he'd sometimes scream and wail so much."

Rebecca was concerned. She didn't want to question her deputy's tactics in front of these witnesses, but she needed to know what had happened inside the house. "What did you find?"

Hoyt shrugged. "Mason was never hurt that we could see. No one was. But he'd get plenty loud, and his dad couldn't always get him calmed down. There were a few times he'd bang his fists on his knees, and he'd bang his head on the wall after we arrived, but he never went after anyone."

"What about his mother?"

Hoyt wrinkled his nose at her question. "She ran off. Which, I suppose, is why his dad placed him in a home."

"When was that?"

"Nine or ten years ago. I don't remember exactly how it all went down. Not sure if I ever knew."

"You think the site's visitor is Mason Alton, and he was confused and thought he still lived here?"

"That's what it sounds like to me."

"Where's his dad now?"

Hoyt scratched his jaw. "Dennis moved out of town years ago."

Rebecca turned back to the construction workers. "Do you have any idea why Mason, if it was Mason, left? Did you chase him off? Threaten him?"

Bloom shook his head. "No, ma'am. Once we realized he wasn't right in the head, we just left him alone and called you guys. He didn't seem violent to us either. But he was loud and ranting, just like the deputy said he'd been in the past. I felt pretty bad for him, truth be told. He looked so distraught. Like he'd lost everything that mattered to him, then someone hauled off and kicked his puppy to boot."

"Sheriff West, what's your location?" It was Viviane Darby, Rebecca's day shift dispatcher and friend.

Rebecca stepped away from the construction workers to answer the radio. "Old Alton Place, now known as The View at Shadow Inlet. What's going on?"

"We've got two reports of a disturbance up at the old Noble Lighthouse."

Rebecca turned to Hoyt, but it was the foreman who spoke up. "Did she say something about a lighthouse?"

"Why?"

Bloom's face paled. "Before the guy took off, he was ranting about the Noble Lighthouse and how that was his real home anyway."

Rebecca frowned. It wasn't the first time the lighthouse had been the focus of attention that day. She remembered reading that today the Preservation Society was supposed to be doing the tour of the lighthouse before arguing their case for renaming it.

All four of them jerked as a blast rang out in the distance. Then another.

Fireworks? Please, God, let it be that.

The Fourth of July celebration was only a few days ago, so kids shooting off some leftover fireworks was a reasonable assumption. But deep in her gut, Rebecca knew they weren't that lucky.

A few seconds later, Viviane confirmed her fear. "Sheriff, update. It's a possible hostage situation with multiple shots fired. The gunshots came from inside the lighthouse, and the door is now closed. There are also reports of people screaming inside."

Shit.

3

Rebecca braced herself on the dashboard as Hoyt pulled up to the lighthouse, sirens screaming and lights flashing. People tried to scatter out of their way but inevitably slowed them down instead. Everyone ran in different directions, forcing them to thread a path.

There were numerous vehicles jammed into the small parking lot and along the grass berm. All of them were empty except one, where a woman stared at them, nodding and talking on the phone.

Any person in the area could be the shooter. It wouldn't be the first time a caller got the details wrong. But none of them seemed to be threats. Instead, they shot terrified glances at the lighthouse as they moved away from it.

Rebecca made note of their faces just the same. A savvy killer might try to blend in with onlookers before slinking away when heads were turned.

As soon as the cruiser stopped moving, Rebecca barked instructions. "Get these people as far away as possible. We don't know if the shooter will open fire, and we need to remove potential targets." She unsnapped her sidearm before meeting Hoyt's gaze. "Once you get everyone to safety, let's regroup behind the cruiser and make a plan."

Rebecca climbed out of the vehicle, using its door as a shield, then took in the scene again.

Civilians started converging on them before the dust had even settled in the gravel, their expressions a mixture of shock and relief.

"They're inside!" A large man in a yellow t-shirt with a parrot on the front pointed at the lighthouse as he jogged over. Sweat poured off his forehead, and he was breathing heavily. The day wasn't hot yet, not truly. And there were no sweat marks on his clothes. This was from agitation. His eyes were wide and kept jumping around.

Rebecca grabbed the man by the shoulder and forced him into a crouched position, mirroring her own actions. "Sir, I want to hear what you have to tell me, but we need to get you to a safer location."

His nostrils flared as he took in his surroundings and nodded. "Okay."

She duckwalked the man into a grove of nearby trees.

"Sorry about that. Did you see what happened?" Again, the man nodded as he took shallow breaths. Rebecca held her hands up to him, motioning for him to calm down. "What's your name, sir?"

"Pete. Uh, Peter Lake."

"Great. Can you tell me what you saw in chronological order?"

His eyes darted around as he licked his lips. "I'm trying to be logical. Not sure what *chrono* means."

Rebecca took a slow, deep breath, motioning for him to join her. "Chronological order. It just means telling me what happened in the order that things happened. So start at the beginning, please."

It was the *please* that got through to him. He gulped and

nodded, then took another deep breath. "I came up here because I heard the view was great and they were thinking about reopening the old place. Wanted to see if I could get a peek inside, ya know."

He waited for her to nod to continue. This was a man who was used to following orders. Hoyt was talking to a woman in a floral sundress who'd also come running up, but Rebecca only had ears for the man in front of her.

"So I saw a couple old dudes go inside the lighthouse. A few minutes later, a younger guy goes in too."

Rebecca nodded. "Go on."

Lake coughed, and she hoped he wouldn't faint before he finished talking. His discomfort with the situation was evident in his sweaty forehead, darting eyes, and shallow breathing. It had to be only his sense of civic duty or morals keeping him there.

"That's when I heard it. A gunshot. Just one at first. But it was followed by a woman screaming hysterically. Ya know."

Rebecca scanned the crowd searching for threats. Her attention jumped over to the lighthouse. The wooden door was closed, and the damn thing looked solid as hell.

"What happened next?"

"Then another woman screamed something about having a gun, then another shot rang out and then the door was slammed shut. There was a lot more screaming then, men and women. And no one's come out since. I called you guys while I hid in my truck. It's been quiet as a tomb since then." He slapped his sweaty forehead. "Ah, man, I wish I hadn't said that." He panted and pointed to an older yellow truck parked in the shade of the lot, next to the trees.

"What did the last man to go inside look like?"

Lake shrugged both shoulders up to his ears. "Nothing special, ya know? He walked out of the trees, over there," he pointed again, this time past his truck, "and I just thought he was part of the group that'd already gone in, maybe running late or something."

"You're doing really well. This is all very helpful. Do you remember anything else?"

"Yeah...yeah! Right before the gunshot, a man yelled something about 'noble.' Then after a little bit, the same voice shouted, 'You can't change the name. You'll ruin it.'"

"Okay, awesome. That's great. Can you tell me what the guy looked like?"

"That's easy. Young, barely an adult. What do they call that, *baby-faced*? Messy brown hair, needs a trim. Wasn't close enough to see his eyes too good. Built, tall as me, maybe a bit shorter. He looked happy, too, like a kid. No. Childlike. I don't know how else to put it."

"Help me understand."

Lake shifted his feet in the sandy soil beneath the canopy of the trees. "Not like a man-child...this is gonna sound bad, but maybe like he wasn't all there. Man's face and body, but a child's expression. *Touched*, like Granny used to say."

Which could mean anything, really. And none of it was good.

Hoyt had finished clearing the area and speaking to the witness and now waited for her behind the cruiser. His eyes were locked on the wooden door ahead of them. Like Rebecca's, his hand rested on the butt of his gun.

"Thank you. That's all incredibly useful." She motioned to the trunk of a massive bald cypress tree. "Why don't you have a seat behind this tree?"

Lake wiped sweat from his face, and she hoped he could get his shortness of breath under control before he started to hyperventilate. Sitting down would hopefully be enough for him to regulate his breathing.

The rattled man practically collapsed behind the natural

barrier. After getting Lake's contact information, Rebecca moved over to Hoyt and rattled off what she'd learned so far.

"Young man, childlike but with a man's body, walked into the lighthouse, yelling about it being noble and they were going to ruin it. Then a gunshot and screaming. After the second shot, the door slammed, and the witness hasn't heard anything since, and he was smart enough not to get close. No one left after the gunshots were fired. At least two hostages, maybe more."

Hoyt scratched his chin. "My witness reported hearing three shots." He nodded at the landmark. "We gonna go up and make our presence known? See what's going on in there?"

Rebecca shook her head. "Not yet. I'm not a negotiator, Hoyt. I've learned the basics, but there are lives at stake."

"I don't think this is Mason." Hoyt shook his head, a twisted frown on his face. "He was never violent. Never used a weapon, let alone a gun."

"We can't know for sure who it is yet. Let's not jump to conclusions either way. Contact his parents and see if they know where he is. He's still got a complaint against him for trespassing at the construction site."

"Like I said before, his mom left when he was little. Took off one day, leaving her husband and kid. No one's seen her since. The dad moved about a year after that. He didn't sell the house until a few years back. I think it was caught up in probate or something, what with his wife's disappearance and all. While it worked its way through the red tape, he listed it for rent. I think he did okay with that, though I'm not certain."

"Any idea why the mom left?"

"Rumor mill says it's because she couldn't take Mason's constant meltdowns. He got a lot worse after she left, though. Maria had always been a calming influence on the kid, so I wasn't surprised when Dennis had him institutionalized. That was about a year after she disappeared. Dennis left Shadow Island after that. Can't really blame him. There were a lot of bad memories on that homestead and nothing to keep him here."

The rumor mill was rarely ever right, though. Rebecca blew out a sigh. Two or three shots had already been fired. The hostages inside were in danger. The only good news at this point was that they'd cleared the area when they arrived to keep the danger from spreading to others.

She surveyed the small parking lot that served both the lighthouse and the Old Witch's Cottage tourism spot, then cast her eyes toward the tip of the island. The Waterman's Memorial was within walking distance, and it had a larger, wide-open parking lot.

Hoyt lifted his hat and wiped the sweat from his brow. "There's no sign, at least not yet, that tells the name of the lighthouse. It barely gets a mention in the *Best Lighthouses in Virginia* guidebook. Not many people know its proper name is the Noble Lighthouse. The tourists all call it the Shadow Lighthouse."

"Well, it could be someone obsessed with lighthouses. There may not be any signs, but there is a website for it. They've been documenting the whole journey to bring back the light."

In fact, they'd just been talking about the news headline spouting that the Preservation Society meeting was today when they'd gotten the call to go out to Alton Place. Rebecca wished she'd somehow had the foresight to bring the paper with her.

Hoyt snorted. "Can't believe we were talking about the lighthouse less than an hour ago."

She couldn't either. "You were so focused on your crossword puzzle, I'm surprised you remember."

He tapped his temple. "Unlike most men, I can focus on two things at once."

She shot him a quick grin. "That means anyone with access to the internet could know they were going to be here today and why."

Hoyt's expression was back to serious when he nodded. "Yep. And that could also mean that we've got members of the Preservation Society and the fundraising committee inside."

Rebecca chewed her bottom lip. "Any idea of the number of people on those committees?"

Hoyt opened his phone. "I'll see if it's mentioned in the article."

While he looked, Rebecca grabbed her radio and made the call. "Viviane, call in all available units, please, including Greg Abner. And ring up the staties. Tell them we've got a hostage situation with at least two people. The shooter hasn't been positively identified, but he might have a history of mental illness."

4

Rebecca spoke with the state police while her deputies worked to secure the scene. Deputy Darian Hudson and retired Deputy Greg Abner finished running the crime scene tape, tied it off, then gave Rebecca a thumbs-up.

On the other side of the tape, Deputy Trent Locke was keeping more people from barging in. Darian had needed to explain to the older deputy to park his cruiser across the road to block it, but not in such a way he couldn't move it quickly.

Greg had rolled his eyes and taken a long walk during that conversation, and Rebecca could've sworn she saw him patting his pockets, like a smoker needing a fix.

The deputies and Greg spread out, walking the perimeter while taking down license plate numbers to compile a list of names for the possible hostages. Rebecca stayed by her SUV, which was in the center of the line of parked cruisers. They were arranged bumper-to-bumper as close to the lighthouse side of the parking lot as they could get, acting as a barrier to shield them if necessary.

Rebecca glanced at Locke, chatting with two pretty young

women while a man walked through the tape behind him. She thought maybe she could use a cigarette too. Locke was supposed to be keeping civilians out while allowing other law enforcement in.

"Deputy Locke, are those two women witnesses?" Rebecca kept her radio near her mouth while glaring at the junior deputy. Her words came out flat and disapproving, and the other three men snickered.

Locke jumped guiltily and looked around in a panic. "No, Sheriff. They were asking for directions to other tourist spots with great views, since I wouldn't allow them—"

"Tell Kaylyn and Jasmine to go back to their homes on Sunrise Terrace." Hoyt managed to make his voice even flatter and more annoyed than she had. "They've lived here all their lives. If they don't know how to get around town by now, your directions aren't going to help them."

"And get back to doing your damn job, son." Greg snapped loud enough into the radio that the two women flinched.

"Clear the road, Deputy. We've got an ambulance and backup on the way. And remove that man you just let through."

Rebecca lowered the radio from her mouth. Hearing that the two curvy distractions were not just locals but lived in the second most expensive area of town made Rebecca's spidey senses tingle. Locke—like everyone else on the force —was working class. The two women were probably members of the upper one percent. Yet they were chatting with Locke like he was an old friend.

She needed to keep a close eye on him.

"If Locke is done ogling the buxom bombshells," Viviane's voice broke in, "Sheriff, the crisis negotiator team has mobilized and they're on their way. They'd like you to make first contact before they get there, since this is apparently a local man, and they could use as much background information as you can get."

Shit. She'd hoped to avoid that.

"Will do." Rebecca didn't let her hesitation carry through her voice. "What do we know about the lighthouse or any people inside?"

Greg took several steps from the perimeter and lifted his mic to his mouth. "Well, if we think it's the Preservation Society in there, that would mean Eleanor "Nora" Weever and Gracie William. Nora's in her early eighties and is president of the group. Gracie's late seventies, I think. There's also Bob Dolan and Chuck…" He snapped his fingers. "Can't think of his last name right off."

"Is that everyone in the society?"

"Nope. The society has a bunch more, but I think there're five on their board of directors. Or maybe there's seven. Not sure, but I do know those four are the most active. Want me to google it, see if I can find more info?"

Rebecca nodded. "Yeah. Find everything you can."

This was taking too long. Rebecca needed to establish contact, no matter how much she dreaded doing so. She took a deep breath and grabbed the mic for the cruiser's PA system.

"This is Rebecca West with the sheriff's department. I'd like to talk to the person inside the lighthouse. Can you come outside so we can discuss what's happened? I'd like to help."

It was a long shot, but she needed to start somewhere.

"No one is coming out!" a man, his voice cracking with hysteria, screamed back. "They need to apologize and fix what they broke!"

What the hell?

"What they broke?" Mirroring the suspect's last couple of words was an active listening skill.

"Yeah. They broke it."

Rebecca tried a different tact. "We had reports of gunshots. Did something get broken because of that?"

"Nooo!" The denial was filled with disdain while containing a petulant-child quality. "Some lady's arm got broken from the gunshot. But she's the one who did the breaking, so that's okay. Now she needs to fix it!"

"What needs to be fixed?"

"The lighthouse!" There was a long stream of indecipherable ranting. "She's supposed to fix it. She needs to fix it and stop breaking it. They all do!"

Rebecca shifted to emotional labeling. "You sound angry. The lighthouse must mean a lot to you."

"It does!"

"I'm glad. The lighthouse means a lot to me too. It's a landmark of this town. Are you local? Can you tell me your name?"

Again, there was a muffled response, and the door shook as something banged against it. For a moment, she hoped that meant he was coming out.

It didn't open.

If this was indeed Mason Alton, not knowing the cause of his mental instability was alarming, as she didn't know how far to push him. Still, she had to keep him engaged in conversation.

"If you'll come out here, I can show you the plans the town has drawn up on how we can fix the lighthouse. The historical committee created a website that explains everything, and the plans have been posted at the town hall for months. Did you see them?"

Come on. Be crazed enough that you forget about self-preservation and just walk out here.

The silence was deafening and wrought with tension. Rebecca looked over at Greg and Hoyt. Neither of them said anything.

"Can you tell me your name? Were you one of the people who signed the petition to fix the lighthouse and get it added to the registry of lighthouses for our state?"

"I didn't see a petition. I...I wasn't out yet. I just got out. But I heard they were going to take the lighthouse away from me. I can't let them do that!"

That was curious.

"Take it away?"

"Yes! My name is Mason Noble Alton, but this is still my lighthouse. This is my mother's leg-a-see to me, and you can't take it away. I had to hurt them to get them to listen."

Hurt them? That isn't good, but at least we've confirmed his identity.

Rebecca texted Viviane, asking her to pull up any research on Mason Alton's lineage, especially his mother's side. She also instructed Viviane to alert the team of their suspect's name and that he had a history of mental illness. *Start a warrant request for medical records.*

Rebecca's shoulders tightened, and she took a slow breath. "I'll listen to you, Mason. Can you come out here so we can talk?"

"No. They're listening to me now. I figured out how to get their attention."

5

Hoyt Frost groaned. He thought he'd recognized Mason's voice. It was hard to tell, since the boy wasn't even eleven when last he'd talked to him, but he sounded so much like his father, it only made sense. Both men had a way of drawing out their Rs, which stood out among the islanders.

Sweat trickled down Hoyt's spine. The last of the cooler morning air had faded, and the brutal heat of the midsummer afternoon was upon them with a vengeance. It wasn't just the temperatures making him sweat, though. They'd counted fourteen cars in the surrounding parking lots. Thirteen were local, and one was an out-of-state plate. Almost half the cars they'd run the plates on had already come back to either a Preservation Society member or to one of their family members who'd arrived after the hostages had been taken.

Greg's research had revealed there were five people on the board of directors of the Preservation Society and seven on the fundraising committee, and those were the people who were supposed to be meeting at the lighthouse today.

From what he'd learned, the Preservation Society board was hosting the event and had gotten there early. The fundraising committee wasn't supposed to be at the lighthouse until eleven, though.

If Mason had waited thirty more minutes, he'd have had a bunch more hostages.

Why, boy? Why are you doing this?

Mason's ravings about them wanting to break "his lighthouse" didn't make any sense. Ruining the legacy didn't make sense either. Mason's family name was Alton, not Noble. As such, he had no strong tie to the name and never did. Not in reality, at least.

There had been plenty of rumors about what was truly wrong with Mason when he was younger. Some people said he was schizophrenic. Others said he had bipolar or multiple personality disorder. Hoyt didn't know what to think and didn't want to try. It wasn't up to him to diagnose the boy back then, only to help him and make sure he was safe. It was those rumors that had given his childhood home the name "Alton Place."

"I can't hear half of what he's saying." Rebecca raked her fingers through her blond hair, messing it up as she shook it out. "I'd be willing to bet the things I need to know are the bits he's mumbling to himself while pounding on the door."

The sun was brutal as it beat down on them. Hoyt tried not to think about how nasty the heat must be inside the fifty-foot-tall brick dungeon.

He scrubbed his fingers over his sweaty scalp. "He's most likely beating his head on the door. That's what he used to do when he was a kid. He'd sit there and bang his head on whatever he was leaning against while babbling. His dad put those foam soundproofing panels all over the walls and doors, and stuck insulation tubes to his bed frame. The boy would have terrible dreams at night and wake up everyone banging his head, and they'd have to go stop him."

Rebecca stared at him, and for some reason, he felt guilt, like he had to explain why he'd let a child like that end up here.

"He never hit himself hard enough to leave more than the lightest bruises. Just sat there, bonking his head. Which is why his room got padded. I swear, Boss, I always thought his old man was doing the best for the boy that he was able to."

"Did you see him actually banging his head on things?"

"I did." Hoyt nodded, remembering those heartbreaking days. "And I saw how his poor parents had developed a habit of reaching out to cushion his head. The old man's hands had more bruises than his boy did."

Like any good father would do.

Hoyt didn't get to see his own sons as much as he'd have liked. Zach, his oldest boy, had moved to the Finger Lakes region of New York. And Adam was off at Boston College, pursuing his undergrad.

Mason was about the same age as Adam, but they didn't know each other well. The Alton boy acted up in school so often that he was in detention regularly and never really participated in any extracurricular activities. And he'd never had a chance to graduate.

Hoyt's heart sank as he realized he'd have to locate Mason's father. To let him know what his only son was up to.

"We need to get closer."

Rebecca was worrying her lip with her teeth as her gaze roved around the octagonal tower. It looked like a tourist whose overly tanned skin was sloughing off in sheets. There were two openings at the base—the rickety door and the slit of a window on the other side that was filled with thick, bubbled glass. Despite being old and decrepit, the door was solidly built, though a gap at the bottom was wide enough to allow a small animal to squeeze under.

At the top, just below the metal band of the walkway around the once-rotating light, was another slot of a window directly above the door. It allowed light into the tower, but there was no way to access it from the inside because of the rotted interior steps.

Mason Alton couldn't see out any more than they could see in. At least that was how it looked to Hoyt.

Rebecca shifted her stance, and he knew she was as anxious about approaching as he was. There was no telling what Mason might do and no way for them to see what was happening. He had a gun and hostages. It would be best for everyone if they could keep the young man calm.

"I need to get closer," Rebecca said again, yanking on the straps of her Kevlar vest. "Communication is the only way we'll resolve this." She pulled her hair back into a messy bun before snatching up a handheld radio. "Watch my back."

"Yeah, Boss." Hoyt rested his outstretched arms on the cruiser's door. From the corner of his eye, he watched as Greg raised his foot and pulled a small revolver from his ankle holster.

Moving steadily, Rebecca inched toward the lighthouse, her hands held up, palms out by her shoulders. In one hand, she held the radio so it wouldn't be confused for anything more dangerous.

"Mason, I'm walking up." Rebecca alerted the skittish man so he wouldn't act rashly.

"No. Go away!"

Hoyt twitched at the harsh response and had to ease his finger away from his trigger. He was there to make sure Mason didn't pop out and shoot the sheriff, not to make things worse by getting so antsy he shot first.

"Because I want to hear what you have to say, and I can't

hear you very well through the gap under the door." She was more than halfway there.

"I'm not coming out! You can't make me. I know what will happen if I come out. You'll take me away like you did before. Like what happened to my mom!"

The door started shaking again, harder than before.

Hoyt winced, knowing Mason was most likely slamming his head into the thick wooden slab. And he was already rambling, talking about his mother being taken away. As a child, he'd never accepted that his mother had left them…left him. He'd always insisted that someone else was to blame.

But, dammit, as sorry as he felt for the kid, why didn't one of the committee members rush him while he was bashing his brains out?

Right. A bunch of senior citizens are going to take down an unpredictable armed man sixty years their junior. Get a grip, man.

"I'm not here to take anything, Mason." Rebecca's voice was gentle, neutral. "I'm here to listen to you. Can you tell me how many people are in there with you?"

Rebecca's plan was working well so far. And she was close enough to at least hear him mumbling.

"It's none of your business. If they're here, and I can keep them here, they can't destroy Grandpa's leg-a-see."

His grandpa?

"How are they destroying your grandpa's legacy, Mason?" Rebecca was only ten feet away.

"Where's Sheriff Wallace? He knows the truth. He knows what happened to my mom. Get him to tell you about it all."

Hoyt cringed at his old friend's name. *What did Alden know about this?*

"Sheriff Wallace is gone. He can't come back either."

Although Rebecca couldn't see it, Hoyt nodded his approval as she neatly dodged mentioning another death.

"I'm the sheriff now. You can talk to me, tell me what led

to all this. Maybe a pair of fresh eyes will find something new so we can all make sense of things."

"They put her in the trees," Mason wailed. "They took her and put her in the trees. She didn't want to leave me. They made her go away forever." The door renewed its rhythmic thumps.

Rebecca glanced back at Hoyt. He shrugged. He had no idea what the kid meant.

"What did the trees do to your mother, Mason?"

"Paddy Pearce. Paddy Pearce. He's like my mom. Just like my mom."

Hoyt's eyebrows collapsed over his eyes. He'd never heard that name before. Rebecca was nodding as if that made perfect sense to her, but he couldn't see her face.

"Does anyone else know about it?"

There was a long pause, so long Hoyt wasn't sure the mic was open any longer.

"Jay! Jay Gossard!"

She nodded again. "Jay Gossard, okay. Does he live around here?"

The banging on the door stopped. Rebecca waited a full minute before she called out to him again.

Silence was the only answer.

"Mason, I have a radio I want to give you so we can talk more easily. I'm going to put it right in front of the door."

More silence.

Lifting her chin, she moved forward until she was only a step from the door. "Mason. I'm at the door. Can I hand you the radio?"

Silence.

With a shrug, Rebecca set it down. "Okay. I'm leaving it here. Just press the button on the side if you want to talk or need anything at all."

Silence.

With little other choice, she backed away until she'd retreated to where her deputies were. Hoyt didn't breathe easily until she was back on their side of the line of cars. As terrible as the banging was, he was even more on edge now that it'd stopped.

"The door's opening," someone shouted.

They all looked up just in time to see an elderly man slowly bend down and pick the radio up. The barrel of a gun was pressed to his temple.

"That's Chuck Anderson," Hoyt said.

When the door was closed again, the entire area seemed to exhale a collective breath.

Rebecca wiped the sweat from her forehead. "Do either of you know those names? Jay Gossard or Paddy Pearce?"

Hoyt shook his head, and Greg did the same.

"You say Mason was committed? Let's find out where and see if we can talk to his doctor. Someone has to know those names."

Hoyt nodded and headed for his onboard laptop. Hopefully, one of those names would have answers for why the child he once knew had turned violent.

6

When the Virginia State Police rolled in with a long convoy of tactical vehicles, Rebecca wasn't sure if she was annoyed or relieved. They kicked up sand, dust, and gravel as they shoehorned into place between the lighthouse and the cruisers.

The blatant maneuver of literally getting between them and the situation was not lost on Rebecca, but she stayed calm and held her position. They needed her as much as she needed them.

As the vehicles started discharging a SWAT team dressed in all black, Rebecca ended her conversation with Viviane. Her dispatcher had managed to find a bit of info on Maria Noble Alton. Perhaps Mason's claims that the lighthouse was his weren't so far-fetched.

A man in a suit got out of the C-23 hostage negotiation vehicle that had parked at the end of their row. He headed her way. "Are you the sheriff here?"

"I am."

He stuck out a hand. "Yes. Of course. I'm Agent Eric

Hazzard with the General Investigations Section. I specialize in crisis negotiations."

"Glad to have you here. Our hostage-taker, Mason Alton, commanded the building at ten thirty. There are two hostages confirmed, both elderly, and another two unconfirmed. They're Preservation Society board members."

Hazzard nodded. "Good work. What else do you know?"

"There's been two or three shots fired, based on witness accounts. No status on dead or wounded. Mason Alton was recently released from a mental institution into a group home. We're still gathering intel on that."

"Do we know what's wrong? Why he's doing this?"

"Yes, according to protocol, I made first contact to see if this could be resolved quickly and opened communication by giving him a radio. He claims he's here to protect his grandfather's legacy and stop them from breaking the lighthouse."

That seemed to throw the agent off. He took a step back and frowned. "He's what? Is the lighthouse getting bulldozed? How does that relate to his grandfather?"

"No, there's no plan for demolition. There're actually plans for restoration. His maternal line has the same name as the lighthouse, Noble. That's the only link we know of so far. Two of my men can answer any questions you have on the landmark's history," she gestured to Greg and Hoyt, "and tell you what we know about Alton's childhood. As I said, the link is on his maternal side, and he seems to also be hung up on his mother leaving him when he was young."

Hazzard shook his head. "I'm sick of mommy issues."

Rebecca pointed toward the tall structure. "The lighthouse is going to be remodeled, and there's talk of changing the name to rebrand and repurpose it to bring in some revenue. I've seen the mock-ups for the renovation."

"His mother left him as a child, some kind of maternal

legacy, and changes to a major landmark?" Hazzard rubbed his chin. "Add in mental health issues, and this could get tricky real fast. That's a complicated story, and to be frank, one that doesn't make sense for a hostage situation."

Rebecca shrugged. "Didn't make sense to me either. As far as I know, no one plans to tear down the lighthouse. I don't know why he thinks that's happening."

"Could be because he tried to go home and found that torn down and gone?" All eyes turned to Hoyt. "This morning, he was on the other side of those trees, where his old family home was. He was upset that his home was gone. Now this."

Rebecca leaned against the cruiser. "Any chance you have anyone from behavioral health with you?"

Hazzard sucked his teeth. "No. But I might be able to talk one into joining us. You said you made first contact?"

"I did. But he wanted to talk to the old sheriff, the one who was still in office when he lived here as a child." Hazzard opened his mouth, but she continued. "He also told us to talk to two other men he thought were connected to his mother's disappearance. Jay Gossard and Paddy Pearce. Despite this being a small town, none of my men know the names, so we're working on identification."

As they briefed Hazzard, more officers and SWAT team members piled out of the vehicles and set up. Several of them walked into the woods. All of them were carrying scoped rifles.

Snipers.

Hazzard turned to see what she was looking at and grunted. "Hope for the best. Plan for the worst."

Rebecca turned away from the dispersing troops. "You won't need those."

"Look, I know he's a local and you don't want to face the

fact that one of your own, someone you grew up with, could be a real bad guy."

She snorted. "I've been here for less than a month. That's not what I was worried about at all."

"Oh?"

"This is a tower built to withstand hurricanes, made out of stones and bricks eight inches thick laid two deep with a barrier of sand in between. Last week, it endured the full force of a Cat 2 hurricane, believe it or not. There are only four openings in eight sides. A door and window at the base, a slit window just below the railing, and the opening near the top that leads to the light." She ticked off the options on one hand. "The glass in the windows is ten inches thick. It was poured into place, then the frames were built into the walls."

Hazzard whistled. "They built them to last back in the day."

"The eighteen hundreds, yup."

"Damn." He shook his head. "That's good information. I'll have to set my snipers up in pairs. One to break the glass and one to take the shot."

That wasn't what Rebecca was hoping for, but it was a point of view she understood. Mason Alton had already proven he was willing to fire a gun. She still wasn't clear on what was broken or if anyone was injured or worse.

"Don't forget, there are no lights in there. Once the sun starts going down, you won't be able to see in."

"That works both ways. As cloudy as that glass is, we can't see in, and he can't see out unless he peeks out the door. Then we can get a look inside." He waved one of the men over. "Have SWAT fan out in pairs around the lighthouse. Look for places to secure a camera and mic."

"Boss." Hoyt stepped up next to Rebecca and pointed toward the road. "Dennis Alton is here. Mason's father."

"Well, let's go have a talk with him. Maybe he can help us figure out why this is happening."

Hoyt nodded and led the way to where a man in khaki pants and a short-sleeved, light-blue button-down shirt was standing. Rebecca followed, but most of her attention was taken by the dozens of men running around with guns.

She'd made a point of how thick the walls were, but if things turned south, would those bricks and compressed sand stop the bullets, or would they just ricochet around inside uncontrollably?

7

Hoyt and Rebecca closed the distance between the scene and where Dennis Alton stood. He was a little heavier and a lot grayer than Hoyt remembered, but more or less looked the same.

The older man had been so intent on watching the SWAT team set up that he hadn't been paying attention to their approach. Now that he'd seen them closing the gap, he looked as if he wanted to flee.

"Hey, Mr. Alton, remember me? Deputy Hoyt Frost. We've met a few times before."

"Deputy Frost, 'course I remember you." Alton smiled, but it was weak and sickly looking, likely held up only through force of will. "You helped my family out a lot."

"Dennis Alton, this is Sheriff Rebecca West. She took over for Wallace."

The man's jaw dropped. "Wallace retired? I thought he would die in the sheriff's chair before he left."

Rebecca grimaced, and Hoyt swallowed hard, then blew out a shaky breath. "He died on the job, actually."

"I...didn't hear about that. I'm sorry."

"You know it's your son in there. Right?"

Alton ran a hand down his face. "I'd heard about it, yeah. But I wasn't sure. So I came up here to find out if it was true."

"I'm sorry to say, but it is true. Mason took at least two people hostage this morning."

"Ah, dammit." Alton ducked his head.

"When did he get out?"

"I honestly have no idea."

Rebecca narrowed her eyes. "How can you not know?"

Alton's sigh shook as he released it. "He turned eighteen two years ago. He's not a minor. Once that happened, I no longer got updates on him. He wasn't committed by the state. I had him put in. Last I heard, his treatment was going really well. Before I stopped getting information, he'd been released to a group home because of the progress he'd been making. But we haven't talked much in the last few years."

"Have you talked with him since he's gotten out? Or seen him?"

"Neither."

Hoyt didn't like the sound of that. "Not at all?"

"I called the group home. They said he didn't want to talk to me. But they make sure their tenants have jobs and learn how to function in the real world. That's all I ever really wanted for him." His fingers worried at the buttons of his shirt. "I did everything I could for that boy since the day he was born. When he would accept it."

Rebecca's expression softened into her *I'm on your side* persona. "What does that mean?"

"After his mom left us, he didn't want anything to do with me. It was like something switched in him. He was a handful before then, but after that…he talked about the craziest things. Saw the craziest things."

"Like what?" Rebecca asked gently.

"He…" Alton's eyes shifted, and this time, he leaned

closer, as if he didn't want anyone else to overhear him. "I don't know. He wasn't making sense. Who can recall the ravings of a deeply disturbed boy?"

Hoyt's breathing nearly stopped, but Rebecca didn't even flinch. "He's your son. You can't remember any of the things he was saying?"

"Well, sure, I can. He'd go on and on about missing his mom. It was understandably hard on the boy, knowing his mom left him and didn't want anything to do with him. I'd find him out in the yard. I thought he might get a wild idea to run away, try to find his mom. I was a single dad. It was impossible to keep an eye on him at all times. And as a devoted dad, that scared the heck out of me. He'd sneak out of school, or out of bed, or wander off in the middle of chores. That's why I put him in the home. So he could be kept safe."

"But didn't you think he'd miss his home?"

Alton flinched, even though Rebecca's brutal assessment was kindly given. "Yes."

Rebecca straightened, her expression tightening. "This morning, before coming to the lighthouse, your son went to where his former home used to be. Opened the imaginary door, checked out his room, everything. Of course, as you know, the house isn't there any longer."

Mason's father swallowed thickly and looked away. "I—"

"It was after he realized his home was no longer there that he came up here, pulled a gun, allegedly shot a woman, and took hostages."

"I…didn't know about that. If I had, maybe I could have stopped him before things went this far."

He looked like he was about ready to puke, and Hoyt felt so sorry for the man. He knew what it was like to have to make big decisions for your kids and hope you got it right. It seemed that was what Alton had done for Mason. In his place, Hoyt might've done the same thing.

"Did you know Mason thought his mother did not leave of her own accord?"

Surprisingly, Alton nodded. "Of course I did. He'd mention there was no way his mom would've left him. I think he started creating stories in his head so he could accept his mom was gone. I mean, who would tell their child the truth? That their mother left because of them? Life wasn't easy. Okay, life was hard. It was real hard. I didn't blame her for leaving. Mason…was a different story. He blamed everyone."

"Like Paddy Pearce and Jay Gossard?"

Alton's eyebrows shot up. "Who? I've never heard those names before. Is that who he's blaming now?"

"Mason told us to look into them to find out about his mother."

"I've no idea who those people are or why he would say that. The cops looked." He glared at Hoyt. "It was your department who told me she'd run away."

Rebecca glanced over at Hoyt, who shrugged. That part was true. Given everything they'd found out, that was the conclusion they'd come to.

She opened her mouth to ask another question but was cut off by Hazzard.

"Sheriff West, you've got a phone call!" He held up a phone.

Rebecca leaned closer to Dennis Alton. "Don't go far. I have more questions for you."

8

Bob Dolan stretched his arms and rolled his neck to relieve the stiffness as he kept a wary eye on his captor. His seventy-one-year-old body wasn't meant to sit on the hard ground. And the tension he'd been holding since the Alton kid had taken them hostage wasn't helping his sore muscles. Bob hung his head as he rubbed his knees. Maybe the extra weight he was carrying was more to blame than the disturbed kid flinging around the lethal weapon.

This day was supposed to be a monumental one for the Shadow Lore Lighthouse, or at least that was what they'd hoped to rename it. The island's Preservation Society wanted to change the name to shift away from the old tales locals and tourists liked to spin and instead give the structure a fresh start. With a new name and new "branding," as his granddaughter called it, the lighthouse could generate revenue for the island and be restored to its former glory.

But Mason Alton apparently had different plans.

Having the police outside wasn't as comforting as Bob thought it would be. Why were they spending so much time talking to Mason? Shouldn't they be trying to get them out?

The kid seemed younger than he looked. If Bob's memory served him well, and he liked to think his daily Sudoku had kept him sharp, this kid was an adult.

Except he talked like a kid.

And he really hadn't stopped talking since he'd arrived. After those first shots, he'd hurled their souvenir mugs around, and he and Chuck and poor Nora and Gracie had all taken cover behind some boxes. But Mason's rage seemed entirely focused on the mugs. Although he'd shot Nora, none of them believed it'd been intentional. It was like he wasn't in his right mind.

Is that better than him not meaning to hurt poor Nora?

The stories Mason kept repeating seemed almost like a mantra. They appeared to calm his troubled mind.

Hmmm.

Bob cleared his throat before softly speaking. "Excuse me?"

Mason snapped his head around, and his wild eyes were filled with...fear? "What? What do you want from me?"

Bob soothed his tone. "You know we're with the Preservation Society." When he got no response, he forged ahead. "I'm fascinated to hear about your connection to this magnificent structure. Could you tell me more?"

"Why? You don't care. You only want to tear this place down."

Patting the air with his hands to calm Mason, Bob tried again. "You told us your grandfather was the keeper of the lighthouse. I'd love to get the rest of your history. So we can add it to the tours and brochures. We can keep your story alive for you."

Mason's eyes darted between Bob and the prone Nora, who Gracie was hovering over while patting her hand.

"What do you mean you'll keep my story alive? Are you going to hurt me like you hurt my mom?"

"Heavens no! None of us hurt your mom. Please, just tell me…tell *us* your story."

Mason had stopped banging his head against the heavy entry door. Even if he didn't tell his story, at least he'd halted that unsettling act. He turned his back to Bob.

Chuck Anderson shrugged at Bob.

Who knew what this kid would do next?

"My mom was Maria Noble. Her daddy was the last keeper of the lighthouse. When I was a little boy, my mom used to bring me here. She called it our special place."

Bob scooted over a few inches while the kid's back was turned. If he could get his hands on something in one of the boxes, it might serve as a makeshift weapon.

Mason turned back toward him, and Bob forced a smile on his face. In reality, it wasn't hard. He was grateful the storytelling had made the kid's movements less erratic.

"That's so interesting. In all my years on the island, I never heard that. I'd love to hear more."

Mason frowned but started to pace. "When I was a kid, I'd get pretty worked up sometimes. I don't know why. My dad said it was 'cause I wasn't right in the head. My mom said not to listen to him. 'Cept my dad talked a lot louder than my mom, so it was hard to tune him out."

Gracie laughed softly. "My father was like that too."

Mason hung his head, and there was a long pause before he continued his story. Walking to the middle of the floor, he pointed at the ground. "We'd come here and sit right in this exact spot." Craning his neck, he looked at the sky through the glass top that was to be repaired as part of the renovation. "You can see the clouds float by."

The boy's fleeting smile was angelic but didn't last long. Light inside the structure dimmed, and Bob guessed a cloud must have passed overhead.

"Ma and I would sit on the floor, and I'd rest my head on

her lap, staring up through the glass. She said lots of people made fun of the lighthouse or told nasty stories about it. But she said it was a 'source of pride.' Those were her exact words."

Mason lay on the ground as if his mother was beside him, and he positioned himself as he must have as a small child.

Bob's breath caught. Here was his opening. He just needed to get up and leap at the kid, wrestle the gun away.

"Sometimes, Ma'd talk about all the ships that were saved because my grandpa worked so hard. She said all of this would be mine one day. It was my…leg-a-see."

Placing both hands on the ground, Bob willed his body to move. His shoulder popped, sounding like a gunshot.

Mason's head turned, and Bob eased back down the couple of inches he'd been able to rise. If he got out of this, he'd join the gym or start doing yoga.

"That's amazing," Chuck said, drawing Mason's attention. "You must be so proud."

"I am!" Mason lifted his head off the ground before returning his gaze to the glass above him. "Ma told me that one day she hoped this place would be fixed up." He rose to his feet and dusted off his rear end, his gaze sweeping across the pitted walls.

Bob envied the kid's agility. "We want to fix it up too."

Mason nodded. "She said if someone did that, then we could climb all the way to the top." Again, his gaze shifted upward. "Said we'd be able to see the whole wide world from up there."

He lowered his head and rubbed the back of his neck. Mason took a few steps toward Bob and Chuck. He waved the gun, but it was as if he'd forgotten he was even holding it. It was just something in his hand. Not menacing.

"Is that true? Was my mom right?"

"I'm sorry. Right about what?" Bob wanted to keep the kid talking but had been too distracted by the bouncing gun.

"If this place gets fixed, will I be able to see the whole world from up there?" He pointed with his gun-wielding hand, and Bob feared he was going to shoot into the vast area over their heads. Who knew what would happen to that live round when it came back down or ricocheted?

Chuck began to answer but Bob bumped his elbow.

With all the power he could muster, Bob turned onto his side until he was on his hands and knees. He crawled over to the chair and managed to pull himself to his feet.

Some hero I am.

He might not be capable of winning a physical fight, but maybe his words could win the war. "I think your mom was a very wise woman. I bet she's right. But you know what? None of us knows for sure, because this place has been broken for so long, none of us has ever gotten to look out."

Mason looked him in the eye, and for a brief moment, he looked like the carefree young man he should be. "Really?"

"We're all old as dirt, as you can see." Bob forced a laugh.

Gracie snorted. "Speak for yourself, Bob Dolan. Nora and I are in the prime of our lives."

The mention of his dear friend's name drew Bob's attention back to his injured friend. He wasn't sure whether her gunshot wound or her missing oxygen tank was the more serious issue. It didn't matter. Her color was fading, and she spent more time unconscious than lucid. She needed help soon.

Mason's pained voice broke through Bob's swirling thoughts. "That's all I ever wanted. Me and Ma to climb all the way to the tippy top and spend the whole day looking out. Far from my dad. Dreaming about our lives and remembering my grandpa." Tears brimmed in his eyes. "I miss her so much."

"We want that, too, you know." Gracie smoothed her sleeves but didn't leave Nora's side. "We want to fix this place. But first we need to get Nora help."

Bob took a step forward. "Yes. As soon as Nora gets to the hospital, we can—"

"No!" Mason's tears were replaced with a hatred so deep, Bob stumbled back. The young man lifted the gun. "I can't do nothing until my…leg-a-see gets fixed. It's all I have left."

9

I could have gone the rest of my life never coming back to this old dump. The streets were too small. The houses were all faded, and a good portion of them had ugly blue tarps spread out on the roofs. The only spot in town that didn't look sun-bleached and weather-stripped was a garish, teal building. And even that hideous place had a parking lot with more weeds than cars.

If a hurricane wasn't proof enough that no one should try to live on this miserable island, I didn't know what else could get through to the stupid residents.

As if that wasn't bad enough, everywhere I looked reminded me of the old days. The bad days. Most people would see this town and think of Mayberry. Little ginger-headed boys running along with a fishing pole to catch up to their daddy.

But I knew better.

I knew the nasty little secrets this town held. No matter the things I'd done over the years, I could never turn evil enough to run with the sharks that inhabited these streets.

It wasn't like I had a choice, not really. Work was work,

and I had to get it done. I'd rather be anywhere else in the world right now. Instead, I was back here, with the sun beating down on me.

But I knew, in the end, it would be worth it. My work here would all be worth it. I just had to make sure things were turning out right.

Surrounded by dense trees, the tower stood proudly above them all. Today, in addition to the scorching sun, the flash of red-and-blue lights bounced off the worn facade. Watching the little men in their ridiculous uniforms running around, I couldn't help but smile. At least one thing was right.

As soon as this was taken care of, I could leave and never look back. One last job and I was done. Hell, my retirement would be secured after this was settled, and I'd never have to worry about working again. If I didn't want to. Retiring might be nice, but so was my job. So thrilling.

I loved it when a plan came together, and this one was coming together nicely.

I'd spun the kid on purpose, whispering in his ear all the things I knew would set him off. It hadn't taken much. His crazy brain soaked up my misinformation like a sponge.

"Excuse me, ma'am," I asked a middle-aged woman. "Can you tell me what's going on here?" My eyes were wide, my voice whispered and breathy with false concern.

The empty-headed woman nodded, subconsciously mimicking my behavior. No one in these events knew how to act or behave, so I was showing them how. "There's someone in the lighthouse. I heard someone say he's got a gun and hostages."

My jaw dropped as I gasped. "Oh, that's so terrible. What kind of madman would do such a thing? I thought I heard the cops say there was a negotiator here. That means this has to be really bad, right? Who are the hostages?"

Feed them a line, something to call the man, and end it with a question to make them feel smart and important. That was how rumors were fed.

"I heard it was the Preservation Society members. Something about raising money to rebuild the lighthouse."

"Why would a madman care about that?"

She acted like it was the most incredible question ever asked. "I don't know."

Time to sow some seeds.

"Maybe he doesn't want the lighthouse rebuilt?" I moved my hand to cover my mouth. "Maybe he doesn't think it's safe?"

She pressed her palm to her lips too. "It does look like it could fall down at any second, doesn't it?"

I bit back a grin. "I think you're right. I bet it's a danger to anyone who goes inside." I pressed my hands to the sides of my face. "And if it falls, I bet it would destroy that quaint old cottage behind it."

Sure enough, she followed my lead. She pressed so hard on her cheeks that her lips puckered. "That lighthouse is dangerous. It could kill so many children."

A man standing next to us glanced over. He looked like a local, and from the sweat on the back of his shirt, I'd wager he'd walked to the scene. He'd most likely want to prove to this intruding tourist that he knew more about what went on in his community than I did. He joined us.

"Place has been shedding plaster and stone for years now. After storms, locals often complain of finding bits of it in their yards."

"Oh, man, that's gotta be concerning. With the way some kids like to explore, I hope you don't have any curious children."

The man frowned in confusion. Stupid local. "I've got

three kids, and one of 'em loves to get into all kinds of things."

"Ahh, I hear that. My kids are the same and would be so intrigued by the debris and where it might've come from that they'd search all over to find its origins."

I frowned dramatically over the thought of my nonexistent children. "I couldn't imagine my kids in a place like that, though. Could you? It would be so unsafe."

He paled and stared at the building that was surely looking like a giant tombstone to him right now.

"I never thought about that." The woman gasped, staring at the local.

"Some people are saying the old witch has returned and she's punishing anyone who goes in the lighthouse. What if those poor souls…" I placed my hand over my mouth for dramatic effect and to hide my growing smirk before my big finish.

"Witch?" the woman breathed.

I nodded. "Let's just pray everyone makes it out of that cursed tower safely."

Some people might've thought that bit was a little over the top, but I knew my audience. Two women made the sign of the cross while one man nodded and whispered, "Amen."

And just like that, I've ingrained this new perception in their minds. The lighthouse is where people get hurt and die. No one will want to visit there after what happens today.

10

Rebecca leaned against the negotiator's van. "Any updates?"

Hazzard lowered the mic he'd been speaking into for the last hour. He took a long drink of water before answering. "His psychiatrist is on her way now. One of my guys is driving her over."

"That's fantastic news. How long until she arrives?"

"Fifteen, maybe."

Rebecca sighed. Time was of the essence.

"Can we get her on the phone?"

Hazzard nodded. "Which one of your men knew the family?"

"Hoyt." She waved for him to join her.

Hazzard tapped his screen. "Dr. Montgomery, I've got Sheriff West and Deputy Hoyt here."

"I'm on speakerphone? This is very unusual. This whole thing is very unusual. My employer insisted on me coming out. You're telling me that Mason Alton hurt someone and took people hostage? In a lighthouse apparently linked to his family?"

Hoyt stepped closer to the device. "Yes, ma'am."

"There's not much I can tell you. Doctor-patient confidentiality."

"We have his father here, if you need to get approval from him," Rebecca offered.

"That's not enough. Mason is no longer a minor, and he's competent."

Rebecca ground her teeth. "You're saying Mason Alton is competent right now? He knows what he's doing?"

"I can't say that now. When he left, he was. I haven't seen him in more than three months."

Rebecca rubbed her temples. "Did he check himself out?"

"Yes, he was counting down the days 'til his twentieth birthday. He left that day, which would've been back in March."

"Can you tell us what he was committed for?"

"I cannot. But you can ask his father, if he's there with you, as you say."

Rebecca spun around. Alton was still standing there, his head twisting back and forth between them and the lighthouse.

"On it, Boss." Hoyt turned and jogged off.

"We've got his father right here."

"Then he can answer those questions."

"So what can you do for us?"

"I can answer any question that doesn't impinge on his rights." The answer was short, laced with a trace of derision. "I can also talk to Mason. We had a good relationship. Oh, I'm pulling up now."

Rebecca and Hazzard turned toward the road in time to see a black SUV slow to a stop.

She held her radio up to her mouth. "Send them through."

Hoyt made it over with Dennis Alton as Dr. Montgomery climbed out of the back seat of the SUV.

Rebecca kept her eyes on Alton and saw him go pale. For her part, the doctor glared at Alton and her lips went tight. There was clearly no love lost between those two. That was interesting. The doctor had a good relationship with the son but not the father.

"Dr. Montgomery, can you tell me how long Mason has been your patient?"

The woman slid her gaze away from Alton. "I took over for Dr. Dinton when he retired about five years back."

Rebecca wrote that name down in her notepad and underlined it three times. There was a world of nuance in the doctor's tone. She seemed to possess the same strong emotions toward her predecessor as she did Mason's father.

"Mr. Alton, what was Mason institutionalized for?"

"He was self-harming, seeing things, had nightmares, and couldn't sleep. After his mother left us, he would rant and scream about ghosts in the woods. Said they were trying to take him away. You guys had to come out and check on us a few times." Alton pointed at Hoyt. "He can tell you."

Hoyt nodded. "Already did."

"Once he was on meds, he calmed down a lot. He could sleep at night again. Didn't always look like hell."

"What kind of meds was he on?" Rebecca asked Alton but kept her eyes on Dr. Montgomery.

"Sedatives for nightmares and the self-harm. Antipsychotics for hallucinations and delusions. He was like a normal boy after that. Or seemed to be when I'd visit him."

The doctor's mouth went tight, and she pointedly looked away from Alton. She apparently didn't approve.

Rebecca turned to the doctor. "Could his actions today be caused by coming off those meds in the last few months?"

"Suddenly stopping medication like that could lead to violent actions. But that's not something you have to worry about with Mason."

"Because you took him off them when he went to the group home," Alton snarled. "I told you not to, but you didn't listen. You said he was fine without them, but now look at him." He waggled an arm at the lighthouse. "He's taken hostages, and you're the one to blame."

Dr. Montgomery lifted her nose. "I—"

"You see?" Alton yelled. "If he does anything, it's all because of her. She's the one who fought me. Had Mason declared competent, took away the pills that kept him manageable, then set him free when he should've stayed where he was safe. I hope after this is finally over, the judge sees that I was right all along and puts him back where he can get the help he needs."

"So he can sit and drool while watching true crime videos all day?" the doctor snapped back. Then she clamped her mouth shut tight against whatever words might be following.

"Whatever he wanted to watch. Better to watch it on TV than to act it out in real life."

Rebecca opened her mouth to ask another question but stopped when Dr. Montgomery gave her a pointed look over her pursed lips.

True crime videos?

That was relevant somehow. She jotted down another note to check with the staff to see what Mason had been watching and how he spent his free time.

Hazzard wiped sweat from the back of his neck. "Doctor, would you mind trying to talk to Mason? Perhaps you can get him to let the hostages go?"

"I can try."

Rebecca tucked her notepad into her pocket, relieved the agent had suggested what she agreed was the best course of action. "Thank you. Just letting him know that he's got someone on his side out here who could help could keep him calmed down."

The hostage negotiator frowned at Rebecca but handed over the two-way radio. "Just hit the call button and speak."

Dr. Montgomery nodded and pushed the button. "Mason, this is Dr. Montgomery. Can we talk?"

"Dr. Montgomery? Is that really you?" Suspicion dripped from every word, and a shadow passed by the slit window.

"It's me, Mason. I heard you were having a hard time here."

"You always were so nice. That's how I knew you were one of the few people who actually wanted to help me."

Rebecca noted how quickly he sounded calmer.

"I still want to help you, Mason. I want to help you get out of there and make sure no one gets hurt."

"People are already hurt. I had to hurt one of them today."

Rebecca scribbled a note. *Who?*

"Why did you have to hurt someone? Who did you hurt?"

"The lady who runs the organization that's trying to destroy my grandpa's lighthouse. I had to stop her. That's why they have to stay here. So they can't sign the papers that will take everything away from me. They already took so much. My mom, my house, my life, my friends, my leg-a-see. I couldn't lose anything more. I just can't, Dr. M."

Dr. Montgomery frowned. "Did the lady you hurt take your mom?"

"No. The trees! They took my mom. Everyone said they didn't, but I saw it. I saw the trees take my mom. But no one would believe me!"

A long, frustrated scream rang out that they'd surely have heard without the aid of the radio.

The gathered crowd at the tape started muttering and shifting.

The SWAT members at the lighthouse looked to Agent Hazzard for instructions. He held up his hand to tell them to wait.

"They said I was just a stupid kid and I was making stuff up! They said my mom didn't love me! They said she left me because I was bad. But that was a lie. It was a lie. The trees took my mom, and…" He tapered off into broken sobs. "I wasn't a bad kid. I was just scared. You know that, Dr. M. You know I was scared."

Rebecca frowned as Dennis Alton took half a step away, as if trying to flee instead of staying to offer comfort and support to his son.

"I know, Mason. I know you were. Are you still scared? Is that why you're doing this?"

"I have to have roots. Roots like the trees. If I don't have roots, I'll blow away in the wind. If I stay in the lighthouse, I won't blow away. I'm staying here. This place is the only roots I have left."

Dr. Montgomery was purposefully slowing her breathing.

"I take it you've never heard him talking like that before?"

"I-I, well…what Mason and I discussed during our sessions isn't something I can disclose."

"What do you think, Doctor?" Hazzard waved his hand at the radio.

"He's completely lucid. He knows what he's doing."

"Do you know what he's talking about, saying the trees took his mother?"

"Again," she pressed her fingertips to her temples, "I can't disclose those privileged conversations." But once again, the doctor gave Rebecca a penetrating stare.

So the good doctor had heard about the trees before and she still deemed him lucid.

The clock could be ticking for a wounded hostage. And to learn that Mason Alton was dredging up old topics from his psychiatric sessions only complicated matters more.

11

Just when Rebecca felt they were making progress by getting Mason to talk, he shut down.

After disconnecting with Dr. Montgomery, Mason was refusing to pick up again.

"Sheriff, what time did you say Mason went in there?" Hazzard didn't look up from his wristwatch.

"First witness reports came in right at ten thirty. Why?"

"And he was at the site of his old place before that?"

"Yeah."

"So by now he's got to be getting pretty hungry. It's been more than five hours." Hazzard grinned. "You know any place around here that has delicious food with an aroma that can be smelled half a mile away? Or maybe, since he grew up here, a place he loved as a kid?"

"Seabreeze Café," Rebecca and Hoyt said at the same time.

Rebecca was quick to add, "Those big juicy burgers and decadent fries make even the most sated person hungry. Make sure you get milkshakes. There's not a kid on this island who doesn't love those shakes, and they come in a big specialty cup everyone knows too. The lid makes a high-pitched squeal when you move your straw in and out of it to suck up the last bits."

Hoyt gave Rebecca a knowing look and she laughed. She'd once made the mistake of walking into the station with a cup for herself but not one for Viviane. It had ended with her milkshake being stolen right out of her hand.

"Let's bring it in. And make it obvious. I don't suppose there's any chance they have a flashy catering van?"

A giant grin spread across Hoyt's face. "A food truck, actually. I bet they can get it loaded and up here by dinnertime."

"You know, I once talked a man down by offering him a cigarette. Comfort is always a great way to talk people out of a bad situation."

"And Betty knows how to turn food into comfort." Rebecca pulled out her phone. "Shall I make the call?"

"Please do. I'll set up my people to cycle through, so there's always someone eating and someone waiting, in case he breaks." Once again, he turned and one of his team came trotting over.

What about the poor hostages?

Maybe Mason would let everyone eat. She sure hoped so.

As she scrolled through her contacts, Darian rushed over. "Sheriff, sorry to interrupt." His dark eyes were serious.

"What you got?"

"I've got Brenda Langley here. She said she used to babysit Mason when he was younger." He nodded to a woman standing to the side. The streaks of blond in her long brown hair were created on the beach, not in a salon. Her outfit consisted of a simple tank top with cutoff shorts.

"Can we verify that with Mason's dad? Make sure she's not just someone wanting to get a closer look."

"She seems to know a lot about him, and everything she's said has matched with what we already know."

Rebecca rolled her shoulders to release the tension before addressing Hoyt and Hazzard. "I say we bring her over and question her. Does anyone have a reason to say no?"

"Langley?" Hoyt craned his neck to examine the woman.

"You know her?" Hazzard asked.

"Not personally. I remember the name as one of the local babysitters when my boys were young."

Hazzard nodded his approval, and Rebecca smiled at her deputy. "Send her over, Hudson." Remembering what she'd just said she would do, she came up with a solution. "Hey, Viviane, you got your ears on?"

"Always, Boss. What ya need?"

"Can you ask Betty if she can send the food truck down here? With all the bells and whistles."

"Is Seaside going to cater?" There was a pause. "To the lighthouse? Where the hostage situation is?"

"I hope so. We're counting on no one being able to resist her cooking."

"Well, if I tell her that, how could she say no?" There was a definite laugh in Viviane's voice, but she kept it down. "You know, if this works, Betty will be telling this story forever."

Rebecca could just picture Betty doing exactly that, hands on hips and chin held high. "Oh, I'm sure. And it will be well-deserved."

There wasn't time for more chitchat. As Brenda drew closer, Rebecca had to refocus her attention as she disconnected. Alton was breathing faster and kept looking away. The sheriff motioned to Hoyt and had him follow her over to meet Brenda halfway.

Hazzard left the doctor and the father with one of the SWAT team and joined them.

"Deputy Frost?" Brenda looked over all the officers standing there and ended on Rebecca. She smiled. "You must be Sheriff West. I've heard a lot about you. That's why I knew I should step up and say something."

"You have something to tell us about Mason Alton?"

"Yes, I babysat Mason when he was little. And he was..." She shook her head. "He was a handful. Always getting into things. Always running out the door. Any door. If it had a door, he ran through it. Always doing something. You would not believe the things he'd put in his mouth. Now mind you, I wasn't babysitting a two-year-old."

"How old was he?"

"When I started, he was six. They wanted an older babysitter, since Mason had some issues. I babysat him off and on 'til he was sent away. He was almost eleven then. It was the year after his mom left. His parents always needed extra help to keep him controlled and safe. His dad needed me even more after Ms. Maria left. I knew he couldn't really afford it. Most of the time, I did it for free."

"*Controlled* or *safe*?" Rebecca stressed each word. Alton had mentioned controlling his son. Which seemed strange to her. She wasn't a parent, but she didn't think most parents thought of their children in that manner. In domestic events, it was an indicator of abuse.

Brenda stopped and thought that over. "Both, I guess? Like I said, he was a handful. He could be up a tree and hiding before you could blink twice. I was just glad his folks didn't live any closer to the beach. If they did, they would've lost him a long time ago." She shifted uncomfortably. "Bad as it sounds, maybe that would've been better for everyone."

The confession sent a jolt through Rebecca. How could anyone think like that?

"Do you think that's why his mother left?" She struggled to keep her annoyance out of the question.

"That's what everyone else said." An array of emotions flashed across Brenda's face. Rebecca thought guilt was one of them. "I heard the stories, same as everyone. He was never that bad for me, but you know some kids only really act out when it's just family around. I have to guess that's what he did. He'd bang pots, his head, and even pots *on* his head, and never napped. He was a nightmare to get to sleep too. I'd have to sit beside his bed until he fell asleep. It wasn't bad, with all the cushions his mama stuck all over his room."

"His mom?" Rebecca scanned her memory. "I thought his dad did that."

Brenda shook her head. "There were a lot of them. But I never saw Mr. Alton do it, only Ms. Maria."

"Do you think his mom left of her own volition?" Rebecca asked, watching Brenda carefully.

"Look, I was barely an adult back then. Only twenty. I'm sure I missed the signs that everyone else saw. But to me," she grimaced, "she looked like the loving mom of an overexuberant boy. Tired and worried, but she would light up every time she came home and hugged him. I do know, without a doubt, that Mason loved his mama. He was always making her little things, cards, crafts, figures out of sticks. He even tried to crochet her a scarf once."

Rebecca softened. "Sounds like you liked Maria."

Brenda nodded. "I did. I was so upset when she disappeared that I helped with the search party. A lot of us in the community did. We walked every bit of ground on this side of the island. We never found a trace of her. There were flyers too. Those got hung everywhere. But I never saw her again. Mason got worse after that. Then he was sent away about a year later. I felt so bad for him. He used to cry for her every night and stopped going out to play."

Hoyt patted her on the back. "I remember the searches. We didn't find a trace. Did Mason ever tell you what he thought happened to his mom?"

"He said she was dead." Brenda's voice was a whisper, and

she wrapped her arms around her waist. "My aunt told me it was probably because he wished she was dead. That it would be easier for him to deal with, instead of thinking she'd just left him behind, like everyone else thought."

And who could blame the poor kid? Who wanted to think they were so bad that their own mother abandoned them?

12

"Oh, yeah. This is when working traffic works out in my favor." Darian Hudson pulled down the crime scene tape and waved the food truck through. As it passed, the side window popped open.

"Hey, there, Darian. You hungry yet?" Grinning, Viviane leaned out of the truck as it pulled away from him.

He jogged after it, keeping pace with Viviane as they headed for the caravan of armored vehicles. "Why am I not surprised you managed to hitch a ride?"

"'Cause you're not just a pretty face but smart too." Viviane took a healthy drink out of a milkshake cup, the telltale screech of the straw straining against the plastic lid bringing a smile to her face.

Darian laughed and slowed down as the truck pulled in where Hoyt directed them. "Doesn't take a smart man to know how addicted you are to those shakes."

"Hey, you said it, not me." She braced herself against the counter as the vehicle rocked to a stop. "How about you help drop the stands while I grab your meals?"

"My meals?"

Betty popped up in the window, pushing the pane open and propping it in place. "You think I don't know what you always order? I made them up while I had the boys load up the truck. If you guys want to use the aroma of my delicious cooking to lure out the bad guy, I needed to have some stuff premade when I got here."

Darian patted his stomach. "No, ma'am, I know how brilliant you are. That's why I'm more than happy to help you get set up."

"Come on, everyone. Dinner's on me."

Darian looked up at the loud call and saw Hazzard walking over. One in every three officers peeled off and made their way to the truck.

Viviane chuckled. "We've got hungry, sweaty people coming for us now, Betty."

"Then you better get your rookie ass out of the kitchen before it gets hot. Go ahead and take the sheriff and her men their food." Betty shooed Viviane away from the window.

As the stabilizing feet for the truck dropped, paper bags rustled and tantalizing smells floated over to Darian, making his stomach rumble. The door at the end of the truck swung open, and Viviane stood holding a tray of cups and two large bags.

Darian finished locking everything into place and reached up. She passed over the first set of food and picked up a second set.

"Those are for Hoyt and the sheriff. And yours, of course. Three milkshakes and a water. I know Rebecca keeps water in the trunks, but these are cold." Viviane carefully stepped down, and Darian made sure she didn't need any help. "Did you know it got over a hundred degrees today? You guys have to be roasting out here."

He couldn't help but chuckle at that before taking a deep pull on the straw sticking out of the chocolate malt. "I had noticed, oddly enough. It's okay, though, I've been in worse." The cold from the drink settled into his chest and radiated through his body, cooling him down a bit.

Viviane raised the bags she was carrying and waved them at Greg and Locke.

Greg shook his head while Locke tucked his thumbs into his belt and pouted.

"They're on second lunch break," Darian explained, leading the way to the sheriff's cruiser. "They got to stand in the shade, so it's only fair."

"Then why are you on break? Weren't you just in the shade?"

"Only long enough to wait on you. I've been standing next to those shiny black trucks all day."

The SWAT team started lining up behind them, orders being shouted.

"Wow. Are those guys always so loud?" Viviane turned, staring at them and glowering at their rude manners.

"They're doing it on purpose, following orders. This is a show we're putting on. Mason can't see us from inside the tower, but he can still hear and smell. So we're using those senses against him."

"Oh. Right." Viviane tilted her face up. "Don't forget to order one of the shakes! They're ice cold and delicious."

She smiled at him around the thick straw between her lips.

"Hey, Boss. Betty made you a strawberry shake. That's your favorite, right?" Darian grinned as he nearly yelled in Rebecca's face.

"Thanks, Darian. Viviane, what are you doing up here?"

"I'm off shift. Melody and I are floating hours this week, remember? Besides, I haven't gotten to see you guys all day and wanted to check on you. I'm going to take the other two their food and drinks. They can at least drink these before they melt, right?"

"So long as they pay attention to everything else." The sheriff sat on the hood of the cruiser and opened her dinner bag.

Darian climbed inside where Hoyt was already tucking into his meal. The younger man sank into the seat, getting blasted by frigid air. "Oh, yeah, that's the stuff." Darian tore open his bag and pulled out the chicken Caesar pita he knew was inside. There was nothing better on a sweltering hot day than crisp greens and creamy dressing. Especially when he had spicy fries and sriracha mayo to go with it.

The senior deputy used one hand to unwrap a burger covered in onion rings while scrolling on the cruiser's computer with his free hand.

"You working or reading comics?"

"Working, of course. This was my first chance to follow up on some of those leads. I'm looking into the names Mason mentioned."

"Paddy Pearce and Jay Gossard? You find anything yet?"

Hoyt nudged the computer screen around. "Nothing on Shadow Island, or even nearby. But I found a Patrick Pearce. He was Irish. And Paddy is the Irish nickname for Patrick."

"Was?"

"I found a missing persons case for him in Norfolk. But so far, I'm not seeing any reason Mason would even know about this guy, let alone think he was involved in his mother leaving him behind. Alton mentioned to Rebecca and me that he was addicted to those unsolved crime videos when he was in the facility, though. Maybe that's where he heard the name?"

That didn't make any sense to Darian. "What? And he just combined the two in his head? Did he go missing the same way Maria Alton did?"

Hoyt shook his head, making a mess as he took another bite of his meal. "Not as far as I can tell. The two cases couldn't be any more dissimilar. He immigrated to the U.S. two decades ago and opened a pub in Norfolk. His family returned to Ireland because their visas expired. They were working on getting extensions, but it never went through."

He pointed at the missing persons report with a picture of a man in his fifties. Patrick was smiling as he leaned against a storefront with the name Paddy's Pub on the glass.

"The report says Paddy was alone in the U.S. He never got married or had kids. His pub was having some financial trouble about the time he disappeared six years ago. They guessed he left to go back to his home country, but they never got a response from immigration and never followed up on it. Do you know if they file the paperwork the same way if someone leaves on their own or gets deported?"

"I'm not sure." Darian wiped his mouth with a napkin, then scrolled through the report to see if there were any names he recognized.

"I think I'll give the detective in charge a call and see if he ever followed up or got a response."

"Why not call Rhonda Lettinger from the crime division with the state police? She seemed pretty competent."

"Yeah, I'll give her a call. I'm going to show West what I found." Hoyt picked up his vanilla shake, opened the door, and disconnected his laptop from the stand. "Don't eat my fries while I'm gone."

Darian nodded and waited until the door was closed before he reached into the bag and pulled out a handful to pop into his mouth.

Hoyt was so busy balancing everything, he didn't notice.

As Darian munched on the hot fries, he wondered what a missing immigrant pub owner could have to do with a hostage situation inside their historic lighthouse. He stared out at the trucks and armed men, trying to put the pieces together in his mind. It was like trying to fit a Rubik's Cube into a round hole. It just didn't fit and wasn't even related, as far as he could tell.

Finally, his curiosity got the better of him, and he got out of the vehicle to pose his questions.

13

"Take a look at this, Sheriff."

Rebecca turned, using her straw to stir her milkshake. The scene was falsely calm at the moment. Everyone was doing as they were told. She'd forgotten how boring hostage scenes could be.

The tactical teams. The waiting. The food trucks. More waiting.

While two-thirds of the agents were hiding and prepared to move at a moment's notice, the other one-third walked around acting like all they wanted was to enjoy a good meal. It was all set dressing to make Mason feel comfortable and hopefully a bit nostalgic. After all, smell was the most powerful memory trigger. Having confirmed with Dennis Alton that Mason had been to Seabreeze as a boy, they hoped the irresistible scents wafting from the food truck would soften Mason's anger.

And make him hungry.

Humans were reciprocal creatures. If they could get Mason to accept food, he'd instinctively want to give something in return. But not even the wonderful smells coming from the food truck had inspired Mason to pick up the radio.

Hoyt had exited the cruiser and moved up next to her as she sat on its hood. He was holding the onboard laptop in one hand and his drink in the other. She leaned over to see what he'd found.

"What do you have?"

Agent Hazzard moved closer to hear what was happening as well.

"I looked up those names Mason told us about."

"Did it lead anywhere?"

"Well, I'm not sure. I only found the one guy, Paddy. But check this out."

Rebecca took the laptop, and Hazzard leaned closer to read over her shoulder. "A missing persons case from Norfolk? We have a contact who can investigate this for us." She scrolled through it, looking for anything that might connect it to Shadow Island or any of its residents.

From what she could see, only one thing stood out. The facility Mason Alton had lived in was also in Norfolk. Other than that, it couldn't be more different. Male, immigrant, business owner who was in debt, had a large family back in his homeland. It wouldn't be the first time someone hopped on a boat to another country and didn't check with immigration before skipping out on their bills.

"What does this guy have to do with our guy in there?" Agent Hazzard frowned at the screen before turning to Hoyt.

"No idea. But this is the name he told us to look into."

"But why?"

"I've got a better question." Rebecca stirred her shake. "How did Mason Alton know this guy's name in the first place? He would've been, what, fourteen when Paddy disappeared?"

Hazzard frowned. "And in his fourth year in the institution. So how does he know anything about Paddy?"

Rebecca took a quick sip, hoping the cold liquid might help her think. It didn't.

"Before we devote too much time and attention to this, find Jay Gossard. If there's something they have in common, then maybe we look into it more. If there's not, it could just be the ravings of a madman." Rebecca made the decision quickly but was already trying to see if the pieces could fit together. "Is there a lighthouse in Norfolk?"

"Cape Henry Lighthouse." The SUV rocked under her as Darian got out and came to join them. "There's two of them at the mouth of the Chesapeake Bay. The other is Old Point Comfort Lighthouse."

"See if Paddy had any history with the lighthouse. Or a legacy to it the same way Mason has with this one."

"Wait, didn't you just tell me to check into Gossard before I looked into connections with Paddy?" Hoyt gave her an exasperated look.

"Hey, I'm just trying to get inside the mind of a deranged man. Don't be surprised if I'm getting a little twisted in my thinking." Rebecca glanced down at her drink. "Honestly, I think I just need some coffee."

"In this heat?" Hoyt frowned and curled his lip.

"Spoken like a true weakling." Darian laughed and clapped Rebecca on the back. "Boss knows how it is. Coffee is life. No matter how hot it is outside."

Rebecca chuckled. In truth, she would much rather be drinking a coffee stout or even a vanilla iced coffee than anything warm. But that was only because she'd been in the direct sunlight all day. Her scalp was starting to burn. Thankfully, Darian covered his high and tight haircut with his standard issue hat, so he didn't have a perpetual sunburn.

"There's two of you. Hoyt, look for Gossard. Darian, since

you know about the lighthouses, check them out and see if you can find anything to link either of them to the names we've been given. Right now, we don't know if this Gossard person is even connected to Norfolk. But as long as you're digging, you might as well look for him too. Focus on their last names, but also check their mother's maiden names, if you can."

Darian nodded. "I can do that from my phone after I relieve Locke for dinner."

She turned to look at the man they were speaking of and noticed that he was once again distracted, talking to a woman. Before she could do more than reach for her radio to berate him, a man ducked under the tape. Without a backward glance, he ran for the lighthouse, carrying a metal cylinder of some kind.

Rebecca dropped her shake. "Stop him!"

Breaking into a sprint, she was aware of pounding feet behind her. But her focus was on one thing. The object in the man's hand.

Long. Gray. That was all she could see.

He was moving like a running back, bobbing and weaving with this package tucked under his arm. A SWAT officer got ahold of him, but the runner managed to shake him off. The tussle slowed him down, though.

Not knowing what kind of gas or propellent he was carrying, Rebecca couldn't risk the object getting near or inside the lighthouse. She dug deep, closing the distance, and gauging her intercept angle.

At least he isn't naked.

"Stop!"

A look of pure horror crossed the man's features when he noticed her approach. He attempted to move the object to his other hand—to block her, most likely.

A second SWAT member came from nowhere, his arms

closing around the man's legs and bringing him down. They hit the gravel with a loud grunt, and the canister rolled away.

Glad to be saved from a gravel rash, Rebecca knelt by the object and heaved in a breath.

"No!" the man screamed. "That's my mom's oxygen. She needs it! I have to get it to her."

It was, in fact, a handheld oxygen tank with a length of tubing wrapped around it that ended in a nasal cannula. Rebecca's anxiety vanished as anger took its place.

"So you decided it would be quicker and easier to provoke the hostage-taker into shooting her instead?" She nodded to the SWAT member whose knee was in the man's back. "Handcuff him and get him behind the cars before—"

"If you don't back up now, I will kill these people! Do you hear me?" Mason Alton slammed something into the door, and the wood shook with his anger. "I will kill them like they killed my mom! Because around here, no one cares who dies!"

"We're taking him away now!" Agent Hazzard called back. "He's not one of our agents. We're not trying to attack you."

Rebecca didn't have her radio on her but turned to face the door. She held the tank out. "It's oxygen for a sick woman inside. Her son wanted to get it to her."

Please, Mason. Please do the right thing.

"Liar! You're a liar! I've seen oxygen tanks! They're as tall as I am, and you need a dolly to move them around!"

Rebecca glanced over at Hazzard.

He shook his head. "I was not expecting that answer."

She hadn't expected it either.

Mason Alton wasn't as stable as Dr. Montgomery had led them to believe.

14

Everything was still going as planned. They were all playing their parts, moving along like the little pawns they were. State and local police were milling around, wasting time, letting the news travel. And it was becoming more daunting by the minute. Rumors were circulating and growing. There was even a reporter wandering about, asking questions of anyone who would talk to him.

"Crazed man-child with a gun wants to destroy the lighthouse," someone said.

Another shook their head. "No, he's been living here since he ran away from home."

On and on.

He killed his mother.

His mother tried to kill him when he was a baby.

No one knew who his mother was, and he climbed down from the trees.

He's been harassing the neighborhood for weeks. Months. Years!

He's a villain.

He's misunderstood.

Mason Alton was a crazy man. The Noble Lighthouse was

cursed. It was so run-down that it could collapse on them at any minute. His dead mother haunted the grounds. He'd been living in the lighthouse alone since he was a child and would attack the locals when they intruded.

Okay, that last one was one I'd started. But the chirpy surfer boy was more than happy to repeat it to everyone he talked to and was even live streaming the story of the Lighthouse Boy of Shadow Island.

I hadn't checked on any news channels yet, but I could just imagine them doing their little countdowns. Somewhere out there, a stiff-faced, middle-aged man was saying, *"We're now in hour seven of the standoff."*

Oh, it was so brilliant.

And that was just on the television. I glanced around and at least half the people gathered were holding up their phones. This was going to be on every social media site. Probably go viral, if it hadn't already. Lookie-loos whispering into their phones, spreading the outrageous rumors I'd pushed.

It was hard to stay out of the view of those cameras, but I just kept my cap pulled low and shuffled around asking more questions like, "Are the rumors I heard true?" No one had told me I was wrong.

Even if I'd just made the story up on the spot, they would nod along and respond with some variation of, "Yeah, that's what I heard too." No one wanted to admit ignorance.

Spreading chaos was the best way to hide the truth. If I spread enough rumors to a wide enough variety of people, even trained investigators wouldn't be able to figure out what the reality was after I reshaped people's memories of the event.

Having this kid create this kind of drama was the easiest way to ensure the lighthouse would be torn down, sooner versus later. That was the best part. No one wanted to have a run-down building in their town that was so dangerous it made national news. They especially didn't want one that would have danger-seeking idiots flocking to it to find out if the internet rumor they'd heard was real.

That was how all magicians did it. *Watch my hand, so you don't notice what's actually happening in front of you. Look over there!*

I nearly laughed. This was going to be one of the easiest tricks I'd ever accomplished. I didn't even have to get my hands dirty on this job.

All Mason had to do now was last a few more hours, and everything would be set. I checked the time. It was already after six. So far, the only problem was that the fool hadn't asked for water or food, even after the cops had brought in that food truck.

Could he hold out without provisions?

Maybe there was food and water inside? I knew that some boxes had been delivered for the committee over the last few days. That had played into my plan, as well, but I hadn't gotten to check what the contents of those deliveries were. Hopefully, the ones with products bearing the new name were in there. That was sure to drive Mason insane. He'd been so proud of having the same name as the lighthouse.

It'd been incredibly hot today. And muggy. To be honest, I'd been surprised at the number of witnesses willing to hang out here for so long. Of course, they weren't really witnesses. Yet. But they would be in the days to come for what was going to happen. And they all sensed it too.

Which was why they were staying. Not to be helpful, but to later boast that they'd seen everything with their own eyes. They all wanted this to end in bloodshed and violence, just like I did. And they all hoped they could benefit from having front-row seats to the show.

I watched yet another guy pushing his way through the crowd. It'd happened several times already. As the people in front got tired, newer, fresher people would step up. This was just another guy taking advantage of the young deputy getting distracted by the woman he was talking to. Half the other cops were busy too.

Not with what was happening inside but with their shift change for a dinner break. No one had seen either hide or hair of the hostages since this whole thing started. And it wouldn't matter if they ever did. Though it'd be nice to have some pictures of poor, beat-up old folks. A shot of the gorefest inside the tower would work too. With this many people, I was certain someone would get a snapshot of the inside once the cops finally gave up and broke in.

That was when I noticed that one guy in the front was holding a bag. It wasn't a purse or a messenger bag, but narrow and blue with a nylon strap. Whatever was inside that strangely shaped bag also appeared to be heavy. He pulled something out, and I tried to get closer to him to see what it was.

I couldn't let my movements catch anyone's attention, though, so I had to make my way over casually. The object he'd pulled out was a metal bottle of some kind. A bomb?

If it was, that would make things so much better.

The guy with the bag looked at the deputy, who was still distracted, then over to where the locals were all gathered around one SUV. I looked too.

Sheriff West, the hostage negotiator, and her deputies were standing around, eating and talking. One of them held a laptop and was pointing at something on it. The sheriff looked over and her eyes widened. I had a moment of unease as I wondered if she'd somehow figured out who I was.

But it wasn't me who'd caught her attention. I was still watching them and didn't see the guy with the bomb or whatever bolt. It wasn't until the people around him gasped that I looked back.

That man was running full speed toward the lighthouse, the metal object tucked under an arm.

What the hell?

Everything was happening so fast. I couldn't keep up.

Stop him.

When the man was finally on the ground, I let out my breath.

The man had come so close to screwing up everything. It'd been the devil's own luck that the sheriff looked over when she did and managed, with the help of SWAT, to catch the guy.

What had kept them so enthralled? I saw the laptop sitting on the ground. No one was looking. They were all focused on the two maniacs yelling about someone's mother dying without her oxygen.

Around me, people were pushing forward. The tape was down, and the sheep wanted to get out to graze. The cops were dealing with the thrashing man and trying to calm Mason down simultaneously.

This was my chance. And I was never one to pass up such a golden opportunity. I stepped forward as well.

Squinting against the reddening light of the evening, I kept my eyes locked on the laptop screen as I sped over to it. I would only have a few minutes, tops.

The pattern on the screen resolved into an outline I knew. A banner at the top with the word *missing*. Then I saw the picture. Rage simmered in my veins.

It couldn't be. No one knew what I'd done back then. No one had even looked into it.

Then I heard what Mason was screaming. He was telling everyone his mother had been killed.

This wasn't good.

None of this was good. I looked around. No one had seen me yet.

Walking backward, I forced myself back into the throng of gawkers. There was no way I could afford for them to take notice of me now.

15

Rebecca tucked in a shirttail that had come loose in her encounter with the man now lying at her feet.

"I've got to find a way to convince Mason we're not lying. Maybe his doctor can help us." Agent Hazzard ran off to talk with some of his team.

Dr. Montgomery hadn't been very useful. Rebecca couldn't fault the woman for her professionalism. Or at least, that was what she told herself. But damn, she could've made things so much easier.

Possibly.

The woman had seemed confused when she'd heard about Mason's mother. Even now, she was standing with her arms wrapped around her waist as she listened to her patient's continuing rants and threats.

And where was Mason's dad through all this? Rebecca scanned the crowd and didn't spot him. *Where the hell is Dennis Alton?*

"Mom, I'm coming, Mom. Hold on, Mom! Just keep holding on." The man continued to kick and squirm as a few officers carried him behind a SWAT truck. "Let me go, you bastards. If you're not going to do something, I will."

SWAT grunted as the prisoner kicked him in the knee, and Rebecca peppered their prisoner with questions. "So you can help Mason Alton push his agenda? Give him an excuse to shoot more people? No, I think we'll just haul you off to jail as an accomplice."

The man stopped fighting. "Accomplice? What? To that guy? He's got my mother in there! Why would I be helping him?"

Rebecca held up a hand. "This is far enough."

SWAT let the man go, and he fell to the ground in four stages, knee then elbow, elbow then knee. He growled in pain as he fell on his back against his bound wrists.

She squatted next to him. "Now, tell me your name, and why I shouldn't charge you with obstructing a police investigation and interfering with a case."

Most of the law enforcement officers were glaring at the man in custody. For good reason. Their hope of coaxing Mason Alton out with food and drink was gone now that he'd been reminded of why he was doing this. Or for the reason he thought he was doing this, at least.

"My mom is in there. She needs oxygen. I brought her the tank when I heard the news about her being locked up. If she doesn't get her oxygen, she'll die. It will be slow and brutal." The man tried to sit up. No one moved to help him.

"If that was true, then why didn't you tell us?" Rebecca snapped. "We could've tried to get it to her instead of pissing off the man holding a gun on her."

The man hung his head. "I'm sorry."

Rebecca didn't feel sorry for him one bit. "If your mother is really in there, you've put her life and the lives of everyone else in there in danger. Immediate danger. Who's your mother?"

"Eleanor Weever. Nora. She's the president of the Preservation Society, and you've got to get her the oxygen tank. She keeps a travel bottle in her bag, but she doesn't like to wear it when she wants to make a good impression. She said…" His face crumpled, tears brimming in his eyes. "She said the tubing didn't match her jewelry and it would make her look weak *and* tacky."

Okay…jackass or not, that was adorable.

Rebecca hardened her heart. "What's your name?"

"Chad Weever. Look, just get my mom her oxygen, then you can question me and press all the charges you want. Her breathing gets really bad on hot days and humid days, and today is both. Mixed with the stress of being held hostage, every minute counts."

Hoyt glared. "Then you shouldn't have wasted everyone's time with your stupid bullshit, you dimwit."

"Get his ID out so we can make sure he's not lying about his mother." Rebecca surveyed the crowd of onlookers and SWAT members. "It's going to be damn near impossible to make any kind of exchange now that you've got him worried about us making a charge on his location. We were trying to get him out quietly using hunger and thirst against him. Or at least get him to trade food for hostages."

Hoyt shifted his feet, and they made contact with the handcuffed man's backside. She knew it wasn't intentional but also believed Hoyt likely didn't have any remorse that it happened. With a shove, Hoyt rolled him over enough to pull out his wallet.

"You've just made everything harder for everyone," Rebecca told him with a shake of her head. She took the wallet and flipped it open. His driver's license identified him as Chadwick Weever, and now she just needed to check who his mother was. She handed it back to Hoyt with a nod.

"I didn't mean to! I just…I couldn't stand the idea of Mom

locked in there, unable to breathe, scared out of her mind, and dealing with who-knows-what." Chad looked remorseful and even a bit panicked. "If they were thirsty, I'm sure they still are. Send them water and food and take the tank in with it. That will work, right?"

"No, it won't work. Mason doesn't trust us and isn't even willing to have a conversation. And you heard him. Because of the way you charged at him with that in your hands, he doesn't think it's oxygen. If you had brought it to us, maybe we could've made it obvious, but not now."

"I wasn't thinking. If I had been, I would've handed it to you. But when I got here from the mainland and saw everything and all the cars and that nothing was being done...and everyone was talking about them being slaughtered and how the place is haunted and how awful Mason is. I lost my mind a little."

"Deputies, get him in the car and run his ID. Verify his story. Once that's done, relieve Greg and Locke. Have Locke take Chad Weever to the station. He can't stay here, and I don't trust him running free. We're going to detain him for now. Hold him in the interrogation room."

That was as close as she would get to blaming Locke where other people could hear, but dammit, she faulted him for what happened just as much as she did Chad.

Haunted? Apparently, he buys into the local lore of the haunted cottage.

"Please, don't take me away. I need to be here!" Chad kicked his feet as he was hauled upright.

"So you can get someone killed? Not on my watch. You can go cool your heels."

"Excuse me, Sheriff West?"

Rebecca turned to find a man wearing a crisp button-down shirt holding out a voice recorder.

"I'm Oscar Toullaine, a reporter for the *Richmond Times*

Dispatch. Can you give me an update on the hostage situation? There are more family members out there waiting to hear what's happening and when they can expect to be reunited with their families."

Unbelievable. At least it's not a camera in my face.

She blew out a breath. "Deputies, we've got one more to haul off."

Oscar blustered, yanking an arm out of Darian's hand. "If you can't talk about that, that's fine. I'm actually here to talk to you about a story I'm writing about an FBI agent who transitioned into the role of sheriff in a small town that's currently being plagued by a crime wave." On that note, the intrepid reporter had the audacity to bare a brilliant, saccharine smile that didn't even come close to reaching his beady little eyes.

"Sir, either step behind the yellow tape or you'll be led away."

"That yellow tape is down. I didn't cross any lines." He thrust the recorder closer to her face. "I—"

"Stepping over it is also known as crossing. Don't make me ask you again." Rebecca turned to find Hazzard. "Gentlemen."

"You heard the sheriff. Let's go." Darian spread his arms wide, shooing the reporter off with Hoyt right behind him as he dragged Weever toward the cruiser to get him safely tucked away where no one else could hear his begging, pleading, and whining.

Searching for the agent and the doctor, Rebecca spotted Hoyt's laptop on the gravel. Another thing to clean up. Sadly, her milkshake hadn't handled being abandoned as well as the impact-resistant electronic device had.

Well, if Betty can't lay claim to her cooking being good enough to stop a hostage situation, she can always say her milkshakes bring all the boys to the yard.

16

Eleanor Weever sat propped up against the cool stucco wall of the lighthouse. Though her arm throbbed, she could barely feel it after she'd woken up. That was probably a bad thing, but it was one she tried not to think about. Gracie had stayed by her side the whole time and explained what had happened while she was passed out.

A man named Mason Alton had taken them all hostage until he could get a promise that the lighthouse wouldn't be destroyed. At first, they'd tried to argue with him, to get him to see reason. But he was convinced they were all liars, and someone else had already conveyed "the truth" about what was really happening.

If she hadn't already been struggling to catch her breath, that would've knocked it right out of her.

What a price to pay for vanity...

If she hadn't been so worried about her looks, she would've had her oxygen tank with her. She'd even bought a pretty bag so it didn't stand out too much. But she'd been so anxious about the cannula making her look weak. Today was supposed to be an important day, and she'd wanted to look and speak her best. So stupid. All these people had already seen her wearing it. What would it have mattered?

"That's all said and done now, Nora. There's no reason to keep beating yourself up over it. Just try to relax." Gracie held her wrist, trying to comfort her or check her pulse, Nora wasn't sure.

Tears welled up in Nora's eyes as she realized her friend was responding to her thoughts. "Was…was I thinking out loud again?"

"Yes, dear. But don't worry about it. Only I could hear you."

They both glanced over to the gunman. He didn't seem to care about their whispered conversation. In fact, he was too busy mumbling to himself, repeating the same story over and over.

There'd been a disturbance outside that'd sent him into a rage just a few minutes ago, interrupting his stories. Someone had been screaming about their mother, and that had incited a tantrum in their captor as he went off, screaming about his own dead mother.

Gracie shifted her grip on the souvenir shirt they had wrapped around the wound to act as a bandage. "And you know I don't mind. We've been friends for so long, I don't need to hear you talk to know what you're thinking. Oh, the shirt is slipping again. I'm afraid I'm going to have to retie it. Can you handle that?"

Already too embarrassed to speak and too weak to argue, Nora nodded. Things were starting to get even fuzzier than before. She wasn't sure if it was from loss of blood or if her oxygen level was too low. Of course, she'd left her monitor in the car, too, so there was no way for her to check.

Nora was reminding herself of the day's events. Little Mason Alton, all grown up, had lost his mind. His loose grip on reality had slipped even further from his grasp after his mother abandoned him and his father. The institution had helped some, but apparently, not enough.

Nora had known Dennis Alton. That man never had a heart large enough to care for anyone, let alone a troubled child. It wasn't any wonder his wife left him. But to leave her young child behind like she'd done just wasn't right.

All of it was just so tragic and sad. For everyone.

A little whimper escaped her as Gracie undid the belt that Chuck had given them to wrap around her arm and hold the shirt in place. Her fingers had been cold before, but now she couldn't feel them at all. To distract herself as Gracie wrapped the leather belt tight again, she tried to wiggle them.

She stared down at the distinct blue color along the cuticles of her right hand. Her fingers wouldn't move. She never painted her nails with color. Her doctor had told her it was an easy way to tell if she was in serious trouble with her breathing.

Nora lifted her left hand to inspect the nails. It was hard to tell in the dim light, but those didn't seem to be nearly so discolored. Still, they were lightly tinged blue. Even though wishful thinking was her brain's default mode, this wasn't because of the gunshot. Cyanosis was setting in. She needed oxygen…and soon.

Her best friend gasped, and Nora had to struggle to focus as Gracie's hand wrapped around her own.

"Oh, Nora. You're freezing. Your breathing is bad too." Warmth poured into her hand and Nora smiled. "I'm going to see if he'll let me get your tank."

Nora's heart rate shot up in fear, and her head spun wildly. She clutched her friend's hand. "No, don't," she gasped, trying to work moisture into her mouth. Earlier, Bob had nearly been shot when the gunman had a dustup with him. She couldn't stand the thought of her friend being injured. "Don't make him angry. I don't want you hurt."

"Nora…" Gracie's fingers tightened on her hand, and they both stared at the man holding them captive.

He still held his gun, an ugly black thing that he waved around as he ranted under his breath. No one else was talking. They were all sitting in their own thoughts and misery.

"If the old sheriff had done his job…" Mason paced to one side of the room. "If that deputy had protected me like he said he would. Why does everyone lie? Is that why they never believed me? Because all they believe are lies? They believed his lies. He always lied and everyone believed him. Lying is bad, but I was the one thrown away, locked up, while they tried to destroy me. Why?"

"Excuse me." Gracie raised her hand. "Nora needs her oxygen tank. It's right out there in her car. If I could—"

"No!"

Nora squeezed her friend's hand as the madman whipped around and shouted at her. He was just a blur against the light coming in through the thick window. It was hard to see again as her heart beat faster. Little dots of black speckled her vision as she tried to pull Gracie back to stop her from approaching the angry man.

She sucked in a deep breath, then another. It wasn't enough, but her vision cleared slightly.

Mason was staring at them both, bits of spittle covering his bottom lip. He must've stormed over at some point, but Nora missed it. The shadow he threw covered them as he loomed.

"No one is going anywhere!"

"But she can't breathe…" Gracie's voice shook, and her hands trembled.

"Neither can my mom. No one cared back then. Why should I care now? And don't tell me lies about how you'll come back either. If I let you go, you'll never come back." He gripped his hair with his hand. "They never come back! You'll leave and finish your plans to destroy the lighthouse!"

Why does he keep saying that?

"We keep telling you, we never planned to destroy the lighthouse. We want to preserve it. Please, no one needs to die."

"Preserve?" Mason Alton lunged forward, and both women cowered.

Nora threw her arm over her friend's head to shield her from the blow, and Gracie threw herself on top of Nora, curling her body protectively.

"Look at this!"

Nora opened her eyes but kept Gracie covered with her good arm.

The Alton boy was holding a coffee mug with the artist's rendition of the remodeled lighthouse and the possible new name.

"This isn't my grandfather's lighthouse! You want to destroy his lighthouse to build your own!"

Frightened out of her mind, she tried to shake her head. "That's not—"

"Save your lies. I know what I'm seeing."

Mason threw the mug, and it shattered against the wall behind them. Nora clutched Gracie and squeezed her eyes tight. The floor seemed to vibrate as he stomped away.

Chuck slowly stood. "We're just a preservation society!"

Mason swung toward him, and Chuck held his hands up to show he wasn't a threat. "No, you're not."

"Yes. We're just locals who are interested in protecting our history. We don't have the power or authority to decide what stays and what goes. That's why we paid to have those things made. We're trying to convince the people in charge to invest in the lighthouse. To restore it to its previous glory.

If you don't believe me, you can look us up online. You can see that we had to do fundraisers and bake sales just to get to what we have now."

As Chuck kept talking, Mason looked more frustrated, but also less angry.

"Your fundraisers raise money to tear down my leg-a-see."

"No!" Chuck flinched as his harsh denial made Mason jerk his gun up. "No. I'm telling you the truth. But I can also show you proof. I'm the treasurer. These others are people who want to help us with our project to revitalize your grandfather's legacy. If you check out our website, you can see our budget. And you can see we can't even afford to hire a crew to mow the grass, let alone demolish a building. It's all there. You can see it for yourself."

Mason raked his hands through his hair, dragging the gun along with it. This was the most they'd spoken since he'd taken them hostage, and he looked more like a lost child with every word.

"If you're not the ones who want to destroy the lighthouse, then who does?"

"I don't know." Mason opened his mouth to start raging again, but Chuck rushed on. "Again, you can look at our website, and you'll see that we're trying to work with the Select Board. You can also see how many other people are working with us to convince Richmond Vale."

"Who's Richmond Vale?" Mason snapped.

"The chairman of the Select Board."

"Then he's the one who needs to make the decision. If he wants to see you people live to see tomorrow, he'll agree not to destroy the Noble Lighthouse!"

"He's a madman," Gracie whispered against Nora's neck.

A child who isn't loved by his village will burn it down just to feel the warmth.

It was an African proverb Nora loved, though she'd never found which country there it came from. The original quote said "embraced," but "loved" was what Nora preferred.

It was true, she realized, as she stared at the grown child who was willing to destroy everything just to hold onto his idea of what should have been. And she and her friends were the kindling for his fire.

17

"Detective Horace, this is Deputy Frost from Shadow Island. I have a hostage situation here, and a name from one of your cases was brought up. I was hoping you could give me a little information on it." Hoyt looked over his shoulder to where the mob of onlookers was finally thinning out as night fell.

"Which case are you needing to know about?" Horace sounded brusque, and Hoyt was sure he could hear papers being moved around.

"An older missing persons case for Patrick Pearce, aka Paddy Pearce."

"Doesn't sound familiar. How old is this case?"

"Six years. There wasn't much to it. A bar owner went missing in the middle of the night. The next week, his bar was foreclosed on."

Horace's tone brightened. "Paddy's Pub. That guy. I remember him, yeah. The Irish man whose entire family had already returned to Ireland. We suspected he did, too, since he had nothing left to keep him here."

"Your report says you never found him. Did you ever find any signs of criminal activity? Anything that might point to him being killed?"

"Killed?" The detective sounded shocked and amused. "Naw, nothing like that. He had an apartment. When we checked it out, some of Pearce's personal stuff was missing. Passport and pictures, gone. All of it looked like it was done in a rush. My take on it was that he realized his last-ditch effort to get a new loan at a lower rate fell through, so he jumped ship."

"Did you track down a plane or boat ticket to confirm that theory?"

"Nope, nothing on the books. But then again, he was short on money too. Yeah, that was the other thing. The safe and registers at the pub were emptied and never deposited. Even a single night's take at a pub in Norfolk would've been enough to get him a berth on some of the less above-board ships that come through here."

"No rumors of him into anything underhanded?"

Horace sighed. "There's nothing viable to prove anything illegal happened. Except that he skipped out on a lot of debts. But that's for the courts and the bill collectors, not the police. Can I ask why you're asking about him? Far as I could find, he didn't have anything to do with your town."

"Well, that's a strange and funny story."

Both men grunted, and Hoyt smiled. Shared pain of the job.

"We've got a man down here who took a local committee hostage to preserve a historical landmark. He claims that your missing man is somehow linked to his mother, even though she went missing about four years before Pearce. Guy down here is claiming we messed up somehow by not connecting the cases."

The Norfolk detective laughed, and Hoyt detected a tired understanding in the sound. "You're shitting me?"

"I wish." Hoyt rubbed his temple. "I gotta ask, any chance your missing man had anything to do with a historical site or landmark or, I don't know, a lighthouse?"

"No, sir. Not around here. Not that we found. His pub was old, but not that old. Plenty of older things around here. We're pretty good at keeping our historical sites well marked and well preserved. We've even still got a cannonball in a wall from the Revolutionary War. But Paddy Pearce didn't have anything to do with that. Unless his great, great, great grandfather was the one who shot it."

"I think the Revolutionary War might be a little outside my jurisdiction, so I'll say that's probably not it." The hair on the back of Hoyt's neck stood up, and he raised a hand to rub it, glancing around. "Is his pub still there?"

"I don't think so. I think it may have been torn down at some point."

"If you remember anything else, would you mind giving me a call?" Hoyt didn't know what he might recall from a case that old, but the oddest things could jog a memory.

"Will do. And good luck with your hostages."

Hoyt hung up and twisted his back. His feet were throbbing, his skin itched from sweating so much, and a headache was trying to settle in from being in the sun all day. To anyone looking at him, he'd appear to be a tired man trying to stretch the kinks out of his body.

But he'd been getting a niggling feeling, one he couldn't ignore. A feeling he was being watched. Clearly, he was being watched by a waning horde of onlookers and some fellow officers. This felt different, though. His mama would have called it the evil eye, and experience had taught him not to ignore that feeling.

Sure, he didn't believe in juju or ghosts or things like that. But every living thing knew when a predator was looking at them if they paid any attention to their gut instinct. That was the feeling he got now.

Common sense would tell him it was Mason Alton in the lighthouse. Except Mason couldn't see out of the slit in the lighthouse pretending to be a window. It was a creepy feeling. He continued to twist, using one of Rebecca's tricks of looking at people without really looking at them from the corners of his eyes.

How the hell does she do this? They just look like blurs of color to me. Getting old sucks. I swear someone is watching me, though.

He quit his charade and stared directly at the group of people on the other side of the tape. Every time he glanced over, the feeling faded. Maybe if he stared at them with intent the same way his observer had been doing to him, he could flush them out or catch them looking. It was about as hodge-podge a collection of folks as one could imagine—men and women of all ages and, judging only by their clothing, from every income class too.

While they looked over at him, it was with the same bored, hopeful expression as the person next to them. None of them were paying him any particular attention.

Then who is? I know I'm not wrong.

Annoyed, he forced his attention to where several SWAT members stood. Their gazes would sweep over him as they kept an eye on everything, but no one stared at him hard enough to raise his hackles. That was when a tiny movement, a disheveled mop of brown hair turning away as he looked, caught his attention.

There you are.

Hoyt left his post and strode toward the man he'd caught staring at him. He jerked and turned his body, moving as if he was going to try to slip away and hide in the crowd. Once he turned, Hoyt jogged to get close enough to stop him before he got away. Everyone was already keyed up, expecting something to happen now that darkness was falling.

Fortunately, the press of bodies was still too tight and chaotic for the other man to make much progress, and Hoyt managed to catch up fairly quickly. Once he was close enough, he dropped his hand on the man's shoulder.

"You going somewhere, Mr. Alton?"

The man jerked and turned to face the deputy with a weak smile. His eyes were no longer boring holes in Hoyt's neck and instead jumped around the scene, looking for an excuse.

"Well, it's getting late. And I've been here for so long already. I was going to grab a hotel room, get a few hours of shut-eye. I'd planned to stick around close when I drove in today."

"While your son is still inside with a dozen cops pointing their guns at him? I figured you'd want to stay at the scene until the end."

"Mason and I haven't been close for years," Alton protested with a shake of his head. "Not since…" His eyes took on a sad cast, but for some reason, Hoyt wasn't buying the grieving widower act this time.

"But you can still answer some questions."

"About what?"

Hoyt wouldn't pull any punches this time. His feet hurt way too bad for that, and guilt had been chewing away at him all day too. If someone had asked him yesterday if they'd screwed up the search for Maria Alton, he would have said no way. Today, he wasn't so sure.

"Why do you think Mason is insisting that his mother was taken by the woods and killed?"

Alton laughed, and it sounded cruel. "Because he's crazy."

"He wouldn't have been let out of the facility if his doctors didn't think he was ready." Hoyt kept his hand on the man's arm as he led him to the cruiser where Rebecca still stood.

"A competent doctor wouldn't have, maybe. But Montgomery did."

That didn't sit right with Hoyt either. While he didn't know the doctor at all, especially not in a professional manner, she didn't strike him as the careless or incompetent type.

"But why the woods?"

"He was with us when we searched for her, remember?"

Hoyt sure did. The boy had been frenzied, and he'd gotten even worse when they'd tried to leave him behind.

He nodded. "I do remember. And I also remember that you're the one who insisted we bring him along because you couldn't bear to leave him alone in that state. Unfortunately, we never found a single clue. In fact, we never found anything to point to why she would've left at all."

Alton shrugged, staring pointedly at Hoyt's hand. "Your guess is as good as mine, Deputy Frost."

Hoyt didn't let him go. "Nah, my guess couldn't be. I didn't love the woman. Didn't live with her, raise a child with her, make a home with her, fight with her."

Alton yanked his arm free. "Fight with her? What are you trying to imply, Deputy? That we fought, and I chased her off? Or that I went crazy and killed her?"

Well, that's an interesting reaction.

Hoyt smiled in the way his wife had told him lit up his eyes, and he laughed. "Of course not. All married couples fight. I've been married for more than half my life, and my wife still picks fights with me about not putting my boots in that weird little basket she has near the door. You learn a lot about a woman from the things she chooses to fight about."

He chuckled again, and Alton lost some of his bluster. "I guess."

"Maria was always putting on her best face around me. Of course she was. I was a cop showing up on her doorstep with a complaint. Even in the best of circumstances, people don't show their true faces to the police. They always feel like they have to keep something hidden. Something she wouldn't bother to hide from her son or her husband."

Alton nodded. "True."

Hoyt lowered his voice, mimicking the way Rebecca went conversational with people she questioned. "That's why I'm asking you. Was there anything we missed? Something to do with the trees around your old house? Or maybe a gut feeling you had at the time that she wasn't acting quite right?"

Alton frowned, and Hoyt could see the man thinking. Not remembering but *thinking* of what to say or how to say it. It soured his stomach.

"Only that her family planted those trees, the cypress that were planted in rows around the house. According to Lucy, Maria's mother, they were planted with the dual purpose of providing income while also serving as a windbreak. Maria inherited that land. We inherited the house, too, and moved in after we were married."

"Inherited? But I thought her mother was still alive. Or am I remembering that wrong?"

"No, my mother-in-law, Lucy, lives up in Virginia Beach. Still alive, as far as I know. She let Maria have her inheritance early because she needed to be in the big city. She's got a heart condition and needs to live closer to the hospitals."

Hoyt couldn't connect the dots. "Has Mason seen Lucy recently?"

Alton shrugged. "I have no idea. Just like I don't know why Mason would think trees killed his mother. Maybe he saw her running through the trees when she left?"

Hoyt would play along. "And his child's mind came up with the idea that the trees forced her to leave?"

Alton nodded eagerly. "Part of his delusions. God only knows what that boy thought he saw. Hell, God only knows what he thinks he sees now. I mean, he took the Preservation Society people hostage because he thought they were going to destroy the lighthouse."

Maybe it was the long day or listening to the rantings of an insane man, but Hoyt no longer believed a word coming out of Dennis Alton's mouth. "But we put out APBs. No one saw her, and we only ever had one possible lead on her car. I can't remember where. Can you?"

The man opened his mouth to answer, then snapped it closed and frowned. "No, sorry. I can't remember."

"Hmm, yeah. Well, I'm sure it's in her file."

"Her file? But surely you have to stay here and get Mason's issues sorted first."

"First? Dennis, no offense, but unless you ask me to look into her disappearance again, I've got more than enough work on my hands as it is without manufacturing more." He patted the man on the shoulder and could feel him relaxing. His next words would solidify Hoyt's growing hunch.

"No offense taken. My wife left me. I made peace with that long ago. I'm sure she's out there somewhere, living a good life with a new husband and kids that weren't as difficult as her first one. I wouldn't want her to see what's become of her son now."

Wrong answer.

Every family of a missing person would jump at the chance to get their case reopened and new eyes on it. Especially with the possibility of new evidence.

"Thanks, Dennis. I knew you'd understand." Hoyt clapped him on the shoulder again and walked over to the cruiser.

Rebecca was talking with Dr. Montgomery, but he was certain the sheriff would want to know just how much Alton was hiding. Maybe talking with the psychiatrist about this new information would help jog her memory.

18

Rebecca had been keeping one eye on Deputy Frost for the last half hour or so. He'd been acting strangely as she talked with Dr. Montgomery. He kept twisting and moving around like he was stretching out sore muscles, and she was getting worried about him. He seemed to calm down a bit when he walked over to talk with Dennis Alton, so she focused on her conversation again.

She was hoping the doctor would have some insight into Mason's personality that would help them coax the man out of the lighthouse and let the hostages go. Hazzard was more than willing to go in guns blazing. Currently, he had his people working to get a camera with sound slipped under the wooden door.

They'd discussed the possibility of employing thermal imaging, but the dense building materials used to fortify the lighthouse against storms were currently shielding the gunman from prying eyes. Once the camera verified everyone's position in the building, they'd be able to make a plan of entry.

Armed entries always came with elevated risks. This was

Rebecca's last-ditch effort to end things peacefully. Normally, this wouldn't bother her, and she would be one of the first to volunteer to make the breach. But there was something about this case that was rubbing her the wrong way. Something about the way Mason talked that made her want to help him.

Dr. Montgomery seemed more than willing to be helpful, but it had been a fine line to walk. Rebecca had learned to make her questions as generic as possible so she could get an answer that wasn't protected by HIPAA. They'd been playing cat and mouse, with the doctor leading Rebecca along with her answers.

Rebecca's phone buzzed and she nearly snarled when it was an email from a reporter instead of the warrant she'd been waiting for. She needed Dr. Montgomery free to talk, and apparently the judge who normally signed her warrants was out sick.

"Tell me, Doctor, do you check up on your patients after they're released from your care? Do they still have access to you?"

"My patients can call me day or night, anytime. They all have my phone number. If they can't reach me for whatever reason, they're transferred to a service that will transfer their call to an associate of mine who has access to all my notes."

Again, there was something in the doctor's voice urging her on. Rebecca was certain if she managed to ask the right question, she would get the information she needed.

"What do the group homes do for your patients? Why aren't they released to their families or left to get their own places to live?"

Dr. Montgomery's eyes lit up, but she didn't smile. "Most patients come to us at a very early age. They have limited understanding of the outside world. The staff at the houses are there to help patients finish their schooling, but they also teach them how to behave as adults in society." She tipped her head forward again, motioning as unobtrusively as possible for Rebecca to continue that line of questioning.

"Limited understanding of how to behave as adults? Does that mean..." Rebecca struggled to find the right word as Hoyt came to stand beside her. He didn't interrupt, but he was frowning and that distracted her. "I'm sorry, I don't know how to say this any other way. Does that mean your patients leave the psychiatric ward not fully adults?"

The other woman blew out a breath and smiled. "They are legally adults, but any person put in such a rigid institution as a minor will be more susceptible to a host of issues once they're released. Not just societal pressures they've never dealt with, but also the stresses of being responsible for themselves. It can lead to them reverting to their previous behaviors. That's why they're monitored at group homes. Places where trained and screened professionals can help them."

"*Reverting*? So they may seem childlike when they get out even though they look like adults."

"That's how many people perceive them, yes. This, of course, leads to the risk that people with bad intentions may be able to sway them more easily. One of the most likely problems is one of our patients falling prey to scams or cults. Because they are used to trusting and listening to people in authority."

Dr. Montgomery was leaning in again, but for the life of her, Rebecca couldn't figure out what the woman wanted her to ask next.

"Especially if they knew that person before and trusted them before they went in. They would also be less likely to question what they're being told."

Hoyt cleared his throat, and Rebecca stepped out of the way. "Are you saying that, say, if someone who was a loved or trusted person from their childhood showed up out of the blue, they'd be more likely to accept anything that person said to them?"

"That's what studies have shown."

Rebecca didn't like the way this conversation was going. That meant that nearly anyone could've convinced Mason that the lighthouse was going to be destroyed. And deliberately or unwittingly convinced him to protect his family's legacy.

But why? The Preservation Society was already working to preserve the lighthouse and breathe fresh life into the relic. Why would anyone feel the need to involve Mason?

Hoyt frowned and chewed on his lip. "What about if it was an abusive parent?"

The doctor smiled this time before she managed to regain her composure. "That would depend on the patient, but it is quite possible."

Rebecca and Hoyt spun toward each other and spoke at the same time.

"Sheriff, you need to hear what I just—"

"Hoyt, I need you to find Brenda Langley, the babysitter, for—"

Dr. Montgomery sighed and frowned at them both.

"We're running out of time." Rebecca turned to the doctor again. "Can you hold out a few more hours? I might need to speak to you again. After I get someone Mason still cares for to talk to him."

"I suppose I can. If you need me to answer any more clinical questions."

"Of course, thank you so much. You can rest in the cruiser. It's not a Hilton, but it'll at least get you off your feet for a bit." Rebecca looked around. It was actually fairly easy to spot the civilians among the uniform-clad police. Brenda's blond highlights stood out like a beacon. "Hoyt, fill me in as we walk."

Hoyt stepped into place beside her. "I was talking with Dennis Alton, and I think he's holding back. It's just a gut feeling right now, but he didn't want us to reopen his wife's missing persons case."

That was odd.

"Families that don't have anything to hide always want the case looked at again, just in case we missed anything."

He nodded, and she was pleased they were thinking along the same lines. "Unless they don't want us to find anything new. He also let slip that the land where they built their house, which he later sold to a developer, was *her* family's inheritance. Land Maria received as an early inheritance from her mother. Dennis never mentioned that back when she went missing."

"But if it's her family property, then why is it called Alton Place?"

Hoyt snorted, and she knew she'd missed some bit of nuance, since she wasn't a small-town girl. Small towns always had their own way of naming things.

"Maria's great-great grandfolks were the first to build a proper home way back before the island was incorporated. After Pops Noble passed, Lucy continued to live in the original home with little Maria. Years later, when Lucy decided she wanted to move to Virginia Beach, she transferred the deed to the land and home to Maria."

Rebecca whistled. "A nice little dowry for her."

"Right." Hoyt rubbed his chin. "Once Maria married Dennis, everyone called it the Alton house. It devolved into Alton Place à la the movie and TV series Peyton Place, once the cops became regulars, shooting them to the top of the gossip circles. People kind of equated the scandalous behavior out there with the fictional show. Before that, I couldn't tell you what it was dubbed. My mom wasn't much for island gossip, and I was too busy hanging around the docks begging pretty much anyone to take me out on the water." He smiled coyly. "But I do recall rows and rows of trees. You wouldn't know it now to look at the place. They were all cleared out for the development."

"Trees," Rebecca murmured. "Taken by the trees."

Her senior deputy swept his gaze in the direction of the old Alton residence. "Since Maria took the last name Alton, that's what people called it. Otherwise, it would have been the Noble Place."

The homestead apparently gained notoriety due to Mason's struggles as a child. Rebecca tilted her head as she thought about the implications of the inherited land.

"Maria went missing ten years ago. That means she would've been declared legally dead three years ago. And the new development is nearing completion on her old land. That seems like about the right timeline for the acquisition, permitting, architectural drawings, and so forth for an upscale community. We need to find out if she had a will or a prenuptial agreement, and what the terms of her inheritance were."

Hoyt nodded. "We never thought there could be a financial reason anyone would want her dead back then. Or any other reason, to be honest."

"Maybe Brenda can clue us into some other reasons." She pointed to where the woman was leaning on the hood of one of the trucks, staring at the lighthouse.

Hearing her name, the younger woman stood up. "Sorry, I just…no one made me leave. And I couldn't stand the idea of Mason being alone here. He has to be so confused and scared." The former babysitter's gaze shifted around, looking at all the weapons.

And I'm hoping you want to do something to make him safe again. Let's see if we can arrange that.

"We need your help understanding Mason."

"Sure." She squared her shoulders. "Whatever you need."

"What can you tell us about Maria Alton?"

"Mason's mom?" Brenda pursed her lips. "She was a sweet woman. Always ready to laugh. She liked it when Mason would tell her jokes. Not good jokes, ya know, but the ones that get passed around on playgrounds. Like, what's brown and sticky?"

"A stick." Hoyt chuckled. "My boys liked telling me that one too."

"Mason would always rush the punch line, so he'd be laughing as he said it. But his mom would laugh right along with him. Now that I'm older, I don't think she was laughing at the joke."

"She was laughing because her son was laughing. And seeing him laugh was the best thing to her." Hoyt's eyes twinkled, and Rebecca wondered if he was recalling a time when his boys were young. He shrugged. "It's a parent thing. We all get it."

"I was thinking more of her as a person. Something that could help us figure out where she might've gone the night she disappeared."

Brenda looked down at her hands, took a deep breath, then looked Rebecca in the eyes. "I've been thinking about it. A lot. That's about all I've thought about since I got here. And despite what everyone said back then...I don't think his mom left him."

Rebecca's heart pumped harder. "You don't?"

Brenda shook her head. "She wasn't the type of person who'd leave. Ms. Maria loved her son. And she loved her land. She had everything she could wish for. If something did go wrong in that family, I think she would've kicked Dennis out first."

"Kicked him out instead of leaving with her son?"

"Right. That was her family's land and legacy. She always said…" Brenda's face went pale as a ghost. "I can't believe I forgot this."

"Said what?"

"She said the only reason she'd ever leave that land would be to be with her father."

Rebecca nodded, understanding the implication after Hoyt's brief Noble family history lesson.

Brenda brushed her hair away from her face. "Pops Noble died right before Ms. Maria returned home after college. Then I think she inherited the property from her mother, but her mom's still alive so I'm not sure how that would work." Brenda searched their faces before continuing. "Ms. Maria said she'd loved growing up there, helping her dad with chores on the farm."

Rebecca's eyebrow arched. "There was a farm on the island?"

"Oh no, sorry. Not a regular cows and chickens and corn kind of farm. The tree farm. For logging."

"Logging? Like commercial logging?"

"Oh, definitely not anything like that." Brenda shook her head. "Have you seen the place? It was small but sustainable. Ms. Maria said even hurricanes didn't mess it up too bad. Cypress trees don't really mind severe weather. They like the extra water and don't care much if it's mixed with salt. And if a few trees fell, she could sell the broken ones, even if they were just limbs. Basically, they only sold trees if they'd come down on their own or if they needed a little bit of income."

The babysitter cleared her throat and Rebecca offered her a bottled water. This poor woman probably hadn't had a thing to eat or drink while she kept vigil for Mason's safe release.

"One day, she asked if I could watch Mason because her buyer was coming by. She needed to collect the downed wood to be sold and hauled away."

"Then why would Dennis sell it after she died?"

"I've no idea. Maybe it wasn't enough to pay for Mason's treatment? I know that was expensive. One night, I overheard him talking on the phone, and he said he was paying a fortune to Mason's doctor. I can't remember his name, though."

To his doctor? Not the facility?

Then Rebecca recalled that the facility was state funded. Dennis Alton shouldn't have been paying much at all. Was he lying back then? Ranting? Or was he paying the doctor directly for some reason?

19

Rebecca rubbed her tired eyes, almost wishing she'd taken Hoyt up on his offer to take a break. They'd need to sleep in shifts, she knew, but dammit, she just wasn't ready to leave, not even for a few hours.

"Hey! Are you guys still awake out there?"

Rebecca was on her feet before Mason Alton had finished the question. His staticky words came through the radio, but thanks to the speaker set up by the state-of-the-art hostage negotiation van, she understood him perfectly.

Just after the sun had set, a team had positioned a camera scope with a microphone under the lighthouse door. They'd tucked it up against the side, hidden in the crumbling stucco. Once that was in position, they'd set up floodlights. Noble Lighthouse was lit up like it was high noon.

Agent Hazzard grabbed the mic. "We're still here, Mason. What can I do for you?"

"It's nighttime, and nighttime means lights out. No talking either."

Hazzard frowned and lifted the mic to his mouth.

Rebecca grabbed his arm before he could trigger it.

"Mason was committed when he was a child. He probably thinks and reacts as a child would. Not to mention, he's been institutionalized and isn't used to the real world with all its complications. Since he left the group home, he probably hasn't had much adult guidance."

"So treat him like I would an adult from juvie?"

Rebecca nodded.

Before they could form a response, Mason spoke again, this time a little bit louder.

"When the sun comes back up, I want to talk to Richie Rich."

Hazzard turned to Rebecca. "Who's that?"

It could only be one person. "I think he means Richmond Vale. He's the chairman of the island's Select Board. If anyone knows of any plan to tear down a town landmark, it would be him."

Hazzard nodded and triggered the mic. "Do you mean Richmond Vale? Why do you want to talk to him?"

"Yes! I want to talk to him because he's a bad man. A bad man!" Mason was screaming again, his agitation growing with each word. "He wants to tear down my lighthouse. My lighthouse! Mine!"

"I thought you said there weren't any plans for demolition." Hazzard lowered the mic and rubbed his eye. "You think there really is some hidden plan to tear it down?"

"I didn't until now. With Richmond Vale, I'd be surprised if he *doesn't* have a plan. He's solely focused on power and making money any way he can."

And control. He wants control of everything and everyone.

Rebecca tapped her phone, pulling up Vale's number. Five rings later, and Vale's voicemail picked up. She gritted her teeth while his pompous voice instructed her to leave a message.

She forced her tone to be neutral.

"Mr. Vale, this is Sheriff West. I'm sure you've heard of the hostage situation at the lighthouse. The gunman is asking to talk to you. He mentioned you specifically. Please call me back so we can get this sorted." She resisted the urge to throw the device.

Hazzard shook his head. "Got any more ideas?"

"If Mason's susceptible to authority figures from his childhood, how about we get his former babysitter over here?" Rebecca pointed to Brenda Langley, who was nervously chewing on her thumb.

Hazzard nodded and headed over to their perp's former babysitter.

Rebecca stayed by her cruiser, trying to piece together the disjointed pieces of this puzzle. A troubled child, a disconnected father, a runaway mother, and a missing immigrant business owner. Plus, some guy named Jay Gossard. And now Vale. What could all these things have to do with each other?

Brenda nodded and went with Hazzard without hesitation. Her fingers trembled as they took the mic. "Mason, buddy, can you hear me?"

"We've got movement inside."

Rebecca perked up at the notification from one of the SWAT members. It was working.

"Miss Brenda, is that you?" There was a quaver in Mason's voice.

Rebecca's heart squeezed for the little boy trapped in a man's body. Trapped in that man's choices.

"It's me, Mason. Long time, no see." Brenda laughed through tears. "Looks like you got into a pickle again, buddy."

"I…I did. But I couldn't think of anything else to do. I love this place. I can't let anyone destroy it."

Hazzard whispered something in Brenda's ear.

She nodded. "Mason, why do you think people are going to destroy it? Everyone who was here today is here because they love it too. They don't love it as much as you do, but they want to see it stick around a long time so their kids can come up here for picnics too."

"Because they told me. I can't tell you who. Shhh…" The hushing sound lasted a full five seconds. "It's a secret. But you know I don't lie. I never lied. People lie, but I don't lie. I hate lies. That's…"

Hoyt appeared at Rebecca's side. She was glad to have him there.

"This is starting to get interesting," he whispered. "Someone told him there was a demolition planned?"

Rebecca didn't understand it either. "As little as he seems to trust most people, who could possibly convince him of something like that? Use and manipulate him?"

Hoyt shrugged. "And what does Paddy Pearce have to do with this?"

She didn't know.

"I know you don't lie, Mason, buddy," Brenda said, validating the young man's feelings. Whether Hazzard was coaching her or if this was instinctive, she was doing a wonderful job. "But I honestly can't understand why you're doing what you're doing either. This isn't like you."

There was a pause, followed by a strangled sound that broke Rebecca's heart.

"Everyone forgot about Ma," Mason finally said. "They said such horrible things about her after she went away. They forgot about her. She was the best mom ever."

Brenda swiped a tear from her cheek. "We haven't forgotten your mom, buddy. We still believe she'll come back to us one day. We've never given up hope. You shouldn't either."

"She won't come back! The trees took her. They took her,

and now there's nothing left of her. Like Paddy and Jay. Like my house and all our pictures and stuff. Like there won't be anything left of Noble Lighthouse. All the meds, the ones they made me take, made me forget it too. For a while. But now I remember. I remember it all."

"Who the hell is Jay Gossard, and why haven't we found anything about him yet?" Hoyt sounded as confused as Rebecca felt.

"She's not gone, buddy." Brenda's voice cracked, and she cleared her throat. "If you still remember her, she's never gone. You still have your memories."

"Unless they make me go back. They could make me take the drugs again. What if I forget her because of the drugs?"

"Then I'll help you remember." Brenda smiled, the gesture coming across in her words. "I have pictures of your mom. Do you remember when we went to the beach, and we buried her in the sand? I took pictures. I still have them." She swiped at her cheeks again. "But, buddy, if you die here tonight, all your memories of her will die with you."

"I know." His words held a world of pain and sorrow. "But if I don't save the lighthouse, who will?"

Hazzard leaned over and whispered in Brenda's ear.

She nodded.

"Everyone who can save the lighthouse is locked in there with you. That's what they were trying to do today before you showed up. Can you let them out so they can finish their job? Then they can save the *Noble* Lighthouse by registering it as a protected historical landmark. Tourists and locals will be able to visit the spot where your grandpa worked. Wouldn't that be cool, buddy?"

The only response was a rhythmic pounding.

20

"I remember Maria," Gracie said, startling Nora.

Mason stopped banging the back of his head on the door and stared at them. "You do?"

Gracie nodded. "She had auburn hair, green eyes, and she was strong as a horse."

Nora giggled. She felt slightly tipsy but better than she had earlier. "Her mind was as strong as a horse too. I'm not sure if I've ever met a more strong-willed person. Not without being pigheaded. Your mama was a woman who knew her facts, wouldn't bend to bullies, and wasn't afraid to let her opinion be known. So you're Maria's boy."

"Yes, ma'am." Mason ducked his head, which was strange to see when he was still pointing a gun at them.

"She and Dennis moved into Lucy's place after they wed. Took over tending to the tree farm, kept it sustainable. They were good people."

"Liar!" Mason slammed his fist on his leg.

Nora was shaken as Gracie jerked back.

"If you thought they were good people, why didn't you help find my mom? Why didn't you help my dad, so he didn't have to send me away? If he'd had more help, I wouldn't have had to go to that place."

"Oh, honey, hush now. You're working yourself up. We were part of the search back then. Maria was part of the community. She'd lived here 'most all her life, 'cept when she left for college. We chatted with her all the time. Shared stories with her about her parents from before she was born. I remember when I told her about her father and how excited he was when he became keeper of the Noble Lighthouse."

Nora paused to catch her breath. Why was she getting so winded when she was just reminiscing?

"We're trying to get this beautiful lighthouse cleaned up and made safe, so kids like you can play here again. Like we did back when we were girls."

Nora rambled on, and for some reason, the boy was staring at her strangely. Gracie's face filled her vision, and she blinked rapidly to try and get her eyes to focus.

"Are you making fun of me?" Mason asked.

"She's not making fun of you, she's burning up." Gracie's cool hand pressed against her forehead.

It felt so nice and soothing. Nora's head hurt something fierce, and her eyes wouldn't focus. Maybe she had a touch of the vapors.

"Why? Is she sick or something?"

Was that Maria's little boy calling to her from somewhere in the dark?

"Because you shot her and refused to let her have her oxygen."

Dear, sweet Gracie.

"That was her son trying to get up here, to bring her an oxygen tank so she could breathe better. Look at all the blood that's soaked into the pretty stucco you say you're trying to save."

Why won't all these people hush? I just need a little nap. Then I'll feel right as rain.

"That wasn't an oxygen tank. Tanks are big!" Mason waved his arms in circles. "I've been in hospitals. You can't lie to me." Mason sounded so angry. He was too young to have so much hostility.

Wait. Is little Mason talking to me?

"Oh dear, my tank is…small." Nora managed a shallow laugh. "I can't…carry…the big bottles. They're too heavy, so I get small ones I wear in a bag…over my shoulder." Nora wanted to gesture to show Mason how she wore her tank, but her arm wouldn't move. "It's been a…life changer…take it with me. Not stuck in my house…that's where I keep the big tanks."

Gracie's warm hand brushed Nora's cheek. "You're so, so hot."

Nora closed her eyes. "Could you…find my oxygen mask? I'm feeling…dizzy."

"Did you really know my mom?"

Nora's eyelids fluttered open, bringing the world back into focus. "I miss Maria. She used to come over…with her baby. And she'd listen…me…hours…talking about favorite hobby…preserving history. Did you know…daughter…last keeper…I have…diaries."

"She needs her oxygen," Gracie cried.

"Sorry. So tired. We can talk…morning." Closing her eyes, Nora tried to tell her friend that she was okay.

"If she doesn't get medical attention, or at least her oxygen, she's not going to make it to the morning. She…"

As Gracie's voice faded, Nora began to float. Past the clouds and farther than the sun. A figure appeared in front of her. Nora smiled.

Mama.

21

Rebecca nursed the cup of coffee clamped in both hands. False dawn was creeping along the horizon, streaking the black of night with streams of grays and blues. The bright lights were still trained on the lighthouse, but if she turned her back on them, she could enjoy the pseudo sunrise.

Hoyt was snoozing in the back seat of the cruiser. She'd just woken up from a catnap herself. As soon as she got out of the SUV, one of the state officers passed her a steaming cup of coffee. They'd taken turns sleeping throughout the night, waiting to see if anything happened.

Mason had sounded so calm talking to Brenda Langley and again later during a conversation they'd overheard between him and some of the hostages. Another negotiator had replaced Agent Hazzard for the night, handling the radio and attempting to communicate with Mason...though the young man hadn't responded.

In light of the information they'd been gathering, they'd decided to take a softer approach and give Mason until dawn. If he didn't turn himself in before then, they'd risk breaching the door.

The stars were still visible, and the grass was heavy with dew. Most of the press remained, but the majority of onlookers had left. It was their absence and the exhaustion most people felt before dawn that had convinced Hazzard to hold out until then.

Lights flashed on the road, and Rebecca picked up her radio.

"We've got a car approaching."

Darian Hudson, who was leaning against a tree but looked to be sleeping, reached up and triggered his chest-mounted radio. "Yes, sir, I see it."

The rough texture of his voice let her know he'd been sleeping. While standing and completely aware of his surroundings. Military members always had the strangest abilities she would never understand.

Tipping himself forward, her deputy approached the sedan as it reached the parking lot. After a few moments of talking, he lifted the crime scene tape so they could pull under.

"It's Vale."

Rebecca snorted. Everyone knew they'd been waiting to hear back from him for nearly seven hours. Darian had said the man's name in the same way she would've said "decaf." As if it were something disturbing and unnatural that you didn't want anything to do with.

Or maybe that was just her cranky early morning attitude putting extra context into his words.

Nah, probably not.

To prove just how right she was, Vale popped out of the passenger seat and smiled like a politician at a rally. Following her instincts, Rebecca reached into her pocket and started the recording app on her phone.

"Good morning, Sheriff West. I just got your voice message and thought I'd drive up instead of calling you back. Wanted to see what was happening with my own eyes."

"Too bad you weren't here seven hours ago, when he was screaming your name and demanding we protect the lighthouse. He insisted you be here, so we'd like to know your role in all this."

Vale frowned, but no way in hell would she offer an apology.

"I'm not at the beck and call of every lunatic with a gun, Sheriff West."

She batted her eyes. "Does that happen often?" She shook her head. They didn't have time for their usual verbal sparring match. "Never mind. Now that you're here, we need information from you."

He glanced at his watch. "Hurry. I have an appointment on the mainland at seven."

Rebecca wrapped her hands around her coffee cup to keep from punching him in the face. "The gunman is Mason Alton, and he believes you plan to demolish the lighthouse. Can you think of any reason why Mason would think that?"

Vale shrugged. "Who is Mason Alton, and how could he have learned about our deal before we've even signed anything?"

Rebecca nearly dropped her coffee. "Are you telling me there's an actual plan to demolish?"

Another shrug. "Not a plan, exactly, but there has been an offer. A very good one. The Lighthouse Luxury Living condo project will bring in more revenue through higher property taxes. Far more revenue than the profit on a few tchotchkes sold to tourists visiting a relic of the past. That's not a deal I could turn down without giving it proper consideration."

Rebecca gaped at him. "And you didn't think to tell anyone? Or discuss it at a town hall meeting? Run it past the

Select Board? We've been out here working under the assumption that Mason was delusional. Have you not been paying attention to the news?"

He polished his nails on his jacket. "I don't watch the news. There's never anything good on it."

"There are lives on the line here!"

Vale waved his hand toward a sniper nest set up on top of one of the SWAT vehicles. "You have more than enough firepower to end this anytime you'd like. Honestly, I can't imagine why you haven't done so already."

"We can't just start shooting blindly. There are people in there."

Either Hazzard heard them talking or had been woken by one of his men, but he walked over to join them.

"Are you Richmond Vale?" He held his hand out to shake.

"I am." Vale smiled and shook his hand heartily.

"About damn time you got your ass out here. Are you a lazy son of a bitch or do you just not take your position seriously?" His glare could have cut diamonds, and Vale snatched his hand back.

"I beg your pardon?"

Rebecca smirked as he tried to puff himself up with his own importance. She knew the truth. Even in a small town like this, Vale was just a small fish. When it came to federal law enforcement, he was below an amoeba.

Hazzard leaned into Vale's personal space. "I said, do you not give a shit about the people you're supposed to be representing, or are you too fucking lazy to answer your phone and door? My team called you all night long and knocked on your door at least twice. You couldn't be bothered to answer, and I want to know why."

For a moment, Rebecca was nearly giddy that she'd had the foresight to secretly record this interaction. This was too good to pass up. Vale stood there, slack-jawed. She needed popcorn.

Is he an early riser or has he been out all night? Ignoring your phone is one thing. Not answering your door when the police are pounding on it in the middle of the night is something completely different.

Sadly, Vale was so put together and clean-shaven, she couldn't tell. Except for the gobsmacked look on his face.

"Are you going to answer me, or should I have my team haul you in for obstructing a federal investigation?"

"I don't appreciate the implications or the tone of your voice."

"And I don't give a damn what you do or do not appreciate. You've kept this situation going for seven hours longer than it needed to. If anyone's died during your delay, I'll see about pressing additional charges against you." Hazzard might be a negotiator who wielded diplomacy like a craftsman, but a large part of negotiating was proving you had the clout to bring about consequences.

The negotiator wagged his fingers, and three state police officers came over, holding their rifles at low ready.

"I'm going to ask you one more time. Why have you been dodging us when we tried to get ahold of you?"

"I haven't been dodging you, or your phone calls. I had an important meeting that ran late last night, then simply fell asleep. I came here personally on my way out of town because I could tell when I saw the messages this morning it was important." Vale tried to sound disdainful, but his eyes kept jumping to the officers at Hazzard's back.

"So you were lazy. Couldn't be bothered to answer your phone when you knew there was an emergency situation happening damn near on your doorstep. No wonder Mayor Doughtie is so preferred to you. He's called up here every hour on the hour to ask for updates and has even visited with the victims' families to keep them calm. Hell, I've had three religious leaders on this island call and ask for updates and to see if they can do anything to help. But you..."

Rebecca sipped her coffee. It had never tasted so sweet. She knew she'd be playing back this recording for everyone at the station later, so they could all get a chuckle out of it. If only she'd secured body cams, so they'd have video of Vale's sour face.

Vale raised a finger. "I—"

Hazzard brushed the finger away. "Tell me what you know about any project that would call for the demolition of this structure and when you started brokering that deal."

Vale straightened his tie, his eyes darting back and forth. "As I just mentioned to the sheriff here, one project is being considered for this location. It would require the run-down lighthouse and that old cottage to be removed. This location would be a perfect plot of land to build luxury condos. Coastal Properties Limited, which operates out of Norfolk, contacted us about this possibility a few months ago. Of course, we were also investigating if this land could be more useful without this eyesore."

Hazzard squared his shoulders. "So profits over heritage? Is that what I'm hearing? Who'd benefit from this addition?"

Vale's nostrils flared. "I am a steward of the public interest. I make my decisions on what is best for the island."

Hazzard snorted. "The island, not the people?"

"If you ask any of our people, I believe they'll tell you that they *are* the island."

Rebecca couldn't keep her mouth shut any longer. "If that were true, then you'd be fighting just as hard to save the lives in there as you're doing to seal the development deal with Coastal Properties." She took a step forward. "It's the people who make this town prosperous. Not the buildings."

Vale narrowed his eyes. "I'll remind you that the island,

along with its residents and taxes, are what pay your salary."

"And my sworn duty is to protect those people and uphold the law," Rebecca shot back. "Not to make the rich richer by profiting off our people and landmarks. Who else knew about this deal with Coastal Properties?"

"Myself, of course, and a few others. The city tax collector, because he had to run the numbers. Representatives of the company."

Rebecca knew the tax collector. He was a tight-lipped old man who would rather sit and commune with a calculator than interact with another person. Under no circumstances would anyone have gotten any information out of him. Not unless the paperwork had been filled out in triplicate and duly notarized.

Hazzard stepped forward. "Who are the representatives of the company, and where can we find them?"

"Carmen Butner from their headquarters. She's the accountant there, I think. And Jeff Benton. He's the one who first approached me with an offer two months ago. I've been working with him ever since."

"And where is Jeff Benton now? Could he have been the one to leak that information?"

Vale went right back to looking like an insulted peacock and primly straightened his tie again. "I can't see how." He waved a hand at his car. "In fact, he's with me now."

Hazzard narrowed his eyes. "Why?"

Vale lifted his chin. "As I've already told you, I have an appointment on the mainland at seven. Jeff is part of that meeting. We're riding together, if that's any of your business."

Rebecca turned to the car just as the driver's side window rolled down and the man behind the wheel smiled and waved. His black hair was thick with gel, and Rebecca felt transported to a used car lot.

Whatever he was selling, she wasn't buying.

22

"Mr. Benton, could you step out of the car, please?" Rebecca walked around to the driver's side, ignoring Vale.

Jeff Benton turned off the car and stepped out. He flashed an even brighter smile than before and held out a business card.

"Is there a problem, Sheriff?" Benton seemed vaguely familiar. Had their paths crossed before?

If Coastal Properties was eager to snatch up the land, it would make sense for him to want to find out what was happening here. Simple due diligence. But Rebecca's intuition was buzzing. Had Vale rebuffed their attempts to reach out to him because Benton was here on the island?

Maybe they were hoping we'd destroy the lighthouse in a hail of bullets?

Nah. Surely not.

"We just have a few questions about why you're here." Hazzard passed the business card to one of his men. "Do you have state ID as well?"

"Of course." Benton reached into his back pocket. "But as

I'm sure Mr. Vale told you, I'm Jeffrey Benton. I'm interested in the future of the island and what my company can do for it."

"Can you step over here, please, so we can have a talk?" Rebecca indicated a spot about ten yards away. Vale took a step in that direction. She held up her hand. "No, sir, you can stay there. We only need to speak to Mr. Benton."

Hazzard passed Benton's ID to the same man he'd handed the card to. "Check him out."

"Yes, sir."

Watching the man walk off with his cards, Benton followed Rebecca away from his car and Vale.

"I apologize for taking you away from your work, but I'm sure you understand how important it is that we understand what's happening here." She smiled at him, and he smiled back.

His expression mirrored hers all the way to the tired eyes. Her smile wilted slightly. His did the same.

Mirroring and matching. No wonder he looks like such a salesman, using those tactics. But I'm not in a position to buy anything from him. So why is he trying to build a rapport by mimicking me?

Hazzard nodded for her to begin.

"We've been up all night, so I hope you won't mind if we make this quick."

"No, of course, Sheriff. I'm sure you've got a lot on your plate with," he wiggled the fingers of one hand toward the lighthouse, "all this going on. Feel free to ask me anything if you think it will help end this travesty."

She barely refrained from rolling her eyes. "Do you live on the island?"

"No, but I've rented a house here for the past couple weeks. Why?"

She ignored the question. "Why are you with Mr. Vale this morning?"

He frowned and looked like he might argue, but the big smile reappeared. "We both have a meeting on the mainland at seven, so I offered him a ride." He winked. "Trapping a client in a vehicle for ninety minutes is a good sales strategy, you know."

Rebecca nearly gagged on the smarm coming from his mouth. "When did you first connect with Mr. Vale about destroying Noble Lighthouse? And how did Mason Alton find out about it?"

Benton blinked, clearly caught off guard by her directness. "I haven't planned to destroy anything. I did a site inspection and realized a few months ago that this land was underutilized and could be turned into something quite remarkable. I approached influential people on the island about my idea in late April or early May. We still don't have any plans for demolition. Nothing has progressed that far yet, so I have no idea how Mr. Alton could have heard about it."

He clearly hadn't heard the conversation they'd had with Vale and didn't know the snake had already told them they planned to tear down the landmark.

Hazzard pulled out a notebook. "You did a site inspection. What was involved in that, and who was with you?"

Benton's eyes darted to the notebook, and he swallowed hard. "I came out here on my own and walked the property. I've been in this business for a long time. That's all I needed to ascertain that this would be a prime location. Can't you just imagine the view?"

"So you didn't need to do soil tests or anything that would require a team?"

"As I said, it hasn't gone that far yet." Jeff's eyes nearly sparkled with arrogance. "That's not how we do things anyway. At least, I don't. I find the perfect property, then the engineers come out to see what type of development is best suited for the area."

Rebecca barely held back a snort. If that was how they did things, it was so they could buy the land at a lower cost. It was like when an uninformed seller listed "artwork" for sale, not even realizing there was a Matisse painting mixed in with the group, and a buyer not telling them the value of the piece so they could get it well below its value and avoid interest from other prospective buyers. It also made the sales go through faster. For a moment, she wondered if she would find boreholes for the soil tests needed for zoning and construction if she went looking for them.

While underhanded, there was nothing illegal about it.

"I'm in Norfolk and have never heard of your company. What's your territory?" Hazzard's condescending tone made Benton bristle at the minor dig.

"In the last ten years, we have several finished sites in Norfolk, Virginia Beach, Suffolk, Manteo, Chesapeake, and Elizabeth City. Half of which I procured for my company. We excel at finding rural or residential locations and turning them into luxury residential ventures. Which is what I'm trying to do for your town, Sheriff."

Ignoring the appeal to her, Rebecca jotted down the names of those cities. Pearce had gone missing from Norfolk six years ago. They were still searching for records for Gossard. They could target the short list of cities and hope for a hit.

"Mr. Benton, how long have you been working for Coastal Properties?"

"I'm proud to say I've represented the company for almost fifteen years now. It's a symbiotic relationship. We make each other rich." His laugh seemed forced.

Hazzard gave a barely perceptible nod at her. He was done with Benton.

Rebecca had one more question for now. "You don't know Mason Alton or how he could have found out about your project?"

"No and no. Sorry."

"All right, if you think of anything else, please call." She handed him her business card. "Since you have business on our island, where are you staying?"

"I've rented a quaint little home for a few weeks. I'm happy to provide the address." With little regard for Rebecca's card, he flipped it over and scrawled the address of his rental, returning the information to Rebecca. "I'd have chosen a nicer place, but your island is quite popular during tourist season." He smiled, and she realized he was somehow trying to compliment her, or at least what he assumed was her hometown and her pride in it.

She opened her mouth to ask another question but yawned instead. She covered her mouth. "Excuse me."

Hazzard yawned, too, his mouth going so wide his tonsils were on full display.

Benton laughed. "Sorry to bore you folks so badly."

Rebecca forced a smile. "Not at all. It's been a long night."

The man who'd taken Benton's ID came back, returning the driver's license to the man. He exchanged a nod with Hazzard.

Benton pulled out his wallet and tucked the license away. "If there's nothing else, I'll let you folks get back to work."

"We'll call if we have additional questions," Rebecca told him.

Benton tipped an imaginary hat and strode away.

Hazzard moved closer to Rebecca. "Did you see that?"

She knew exactly what he meant. "The yawn. Yeah."

Hoyt appeared by her side. "What about a yawn?" He handed them both a fresh cup of coffee.

"Humans yawn in response to other humans yawning,"

Hazzard explained. "It's automatic. I even yawn when I see my dog yawning."

When the agent took a sip of his coffee, Rebecca took over. "Psychopaths have reduced susceptibility or can even be immune to contagious yawning."

Hoyt yawned. "No shit?"

She smiled. "Nope. A study had subjects take a psychopathic personality test and exposed them to a contagious yawn experiment. Turns out, one of the tests on the psychopathy scale is a person's ability to yawn in reaction to another person yawning. The more coldhearted a person is, meaning they're less empathetic, the less likely they're able to catch a yawn."

Hoyt nodded at the retreating vehicle. "Benton didn't yawn?"

She watched the taillights disappear. "Nope."

23

"Who are you, Jeffrey Benton?"

Rebecca hit the enter key and scowled at her monitor as Benton's face appeared on her screen. She scrolled down and began reading the preliminary background search she'd ordered.

Salespeople generally gave Rebecca hives, so she knew Benton's salesman aura could be part of her immediate dislike of him. The yawning thing was interesting, but even if he was a psychopath, that didn't mean he was a killer.

She'd recently read a study that estimated that 1.2 percent of U.S. adult men and 0.3 to 0.7 percent of U.S. adult women were considered to have clinically significant levels of psychopathic traits. But having traits was much different than killing another person. Or manipulating a mentally vulnerable young man into doing it for you.

Hoyt knocked on her window. "Boss, we got a man here who says you know him."

She glanced at the idling black car her deputy gestured toward. It looked familiar, but she couldn't see the driver.

"Yeah, well, if he knows me, he would have brought

coffee." She couldn't help but joke, trying to chase off the goose bumps she'd developed talking to Jeff Benton.

"He's got coffee and a breakfast sandwich." Hoyt raised an eyebrow. "He wants me to tell you it's chicken with cheese and an extra pickle."

That got Rebecca's attention. Chicken, cheese, and pickle on a biscuit was her go-to after a long night of working. "Send him through."

Hoyt radioed the guard, and a few moments later, the car began to move. Who could it be? It wasn't one of her deputies, because they would've just walked up to her and tossed the sandwich in her lap.

Ryker?

A tiny part of her heart hoped it was him, but she didn't remember sharing that specific biscuit combination with him. He also drove a truck.

Stepping out of her cruiser, she waited for the car to park. When the door opened and Benji Huang stepped out, she almost fell over. She hadn't expected her old FBI partner to appear.

He grinned as she stared open-mouthed at him. His black hair was just as shiny as she remembered, but it was quite a bit shorter, with the back and sides clipped close and the top only a few inches long.

Hoyt pointed to his left. "I'll just, um, go over there."

He was gone before Rebecca could answer.

Benji held up a takeout bag, his dark brown eyes glinting with laughter. "I knew I'd find you hard at work. You always were a morning person."

She snorted. "I'm only a morning person if…" She snatched the bag. "Okay, now I can pretend that I'm a morning person." She gave him a brief hug before taking the coffee. "What are you doing here?"

"I needed to get away and heard what was going on.

You've talked about this place before, and it seemed like the perfect time to come down." He leaned against his car and scanned the area. "So how are you dealing with all this?"

Rebecca unwrapped her sandwich, giving herself a little time before answering. "You mean, am I worried about the hostage situation knowing how badly my last one went?"

"I mean, how are you dealing with this hostage situation after how much you blamed yourself for the last one?" Benji was as calm as could be. "You're the only one who thinks you screwed that up."

"I'm doing okay. Believe it or not, I'm working to not accept responsibility for things I have no control over. Therapy helped." She tried not to feel self-conscious, and instead shifted her attention to the warm sandwich in her hand.

"That's good to hear. I was worried about you."

"Because you think I'm going to crack under the pressure like you think I did with the Morley case?" Rebecca failed to keep the bitter tone in check.

Benji, long used to her snippy attitude so early in the morning, kept his eyes on the sunrise. "No, because you were supposed to be on vacation, and instead, you started a new job just days later and took over an entire station on your own with all the admin duties that go with that. This island is so small, can you even get a respectable cup of coffee?"

She laughed. "Hey, we have very good coffee here." She took a bite, groaning as all the flavors melded in her mouth. "Life got weird. I did the best I could, given the situation."

"I know how that goes. Since you left, I had to partner up with Colby."

Rebecca clapped a hand over her mouth. "I shouldn't laugh. I know I shouldn't. But that guy is such a tool. How are you even able to work with him?"

"I do a lot of fieldwork now. Solo work. And I've taken to

wearing earbuds when we're on the road."

"Catching up on your audiobooks?" She relaxed into the nonjudgmental conversation.

"It's a small silver lining on the shit cake you left me with."

"If it makes you feel any better, I have to work with the man that screwed up and got the last sheriff shot, then turned around and spread rumors that it was my fault. And I have to be his unbiased boss."

Benji overexaggerated a flinch. "Okay, Colby isn't that bad. Damn. If you're his boss, why not just fire the guy?"

"No one to take his place. You called it. This is a small town. That means it's a small employee field, too, and honestly, I've had back-to-back cases since I started. No time to hire and train another person." She knew it was a pitiful excuse, but it was true. "For now, I just keep him on nights and check all his work."

"While keeping him as far away from you as possible."

"Whenever possible, yes. I had to call him in yesterday to deal with traffic and monitor this crime scene. Instead, he got distracted by a pretty face and let a man run most of the way up to the lighthouse before I could stop him."

"Jeez, Rebecca, that's not good. You have to get rid of that guy. Seriously. A guy like that can destroy an investigation."

"I know, I know." She took another nibble. "And I'm working on it. But that takes time, and I don't have a lot of it to spare right now."

Rebecca noticed Hoyt glancing her way. Poor guy. He looked worried.

"Come on." She headed in her deputy's direction. "You can meet one of the upsides of working here."

Benji was right on her heels. "Lead the way."

"Deputy Hoyt Frost, meet Special Agent Benji Huang. He's my old partner and came down for a visit. Benji, this is my senior deputy and right-hand man."

Hoyt held out his hand. "Good to meet you, Special Agent Huang. You here for business or pleasure?"

"Mostly pleasure, but I know Rebecca well enough to know she's not going to stop working and will more than likely give me something to do to help her out."

Hoyt laughed, and Rebecca scowled but didn't bother to object. If there was something an FBI agent could do to end this sooner, she wasn't above asking for that assistance.

"Speaking of working, Sheriff, I got to thinking and looked up the missing persons case on Maria Alton. It turns out her mother, not her husband, filed it."

"Dennis Alton didn't file a missing persons report on his wife? Doesn't her mother live in Virginia Beach?"

"Yeah, she's two hours away. I've got her number if you want to talk to her."

Rebecca checked the time. It was a few minutes before six a.m. "It's a little early to call. But she might know something that could help. Better to ask forgiveness than permission." It was one of Rebecca's favorite quotes. "Let's hope she's a morning person. Benji, you want to hang out with Hoyt until I'm done with this?"

"Sure." Benji's grin widened. "I'm sure we can find lots of things to talk about."

Rebecca sighed, knowing what was coming. "You really don't have to…"

Benji slung an arm over Hoyt's shoulder and the two walked away. "Did Rebecca ever tell you about the time she had to chase down a crazy woman with a purse full of mice?"

Hoyt laughed. "Did she tell you about having to tackle a sweaty naked man to the ground?"

Rebecca stuffed half the biscuit in her mouth. If she was going to be humiliated by these two, she'd at least do it on a full stomach.

24

The phone only rang a couple of times before an elderly-sounding woman answered.

"Am I speaking with Lucy Noble?"

"Yes. Can I help you?"

"I hope so, Mrs. Noble. I apologize for calling so early. My name is Sheriff West, and I'm calling from Shadow Island." As expected, she was cut off before she could explain.

"Did you find her?" The fear and excitement in the woman's voice were heartbreaking. "Did you find my daughter? Is she okay?"

"No, ma'am, I'm sorry. I'm not calling about your daughter right now. I'm calling about your grandson." There was no reason for her to get the woman's hopes up by telling her they were going to be reopening her daughter's case.

"Mason? What's wrong with Mason? I can be over at his facility in twenty minutes." Dishes clattered and slippers scurried as commotion ensued on the other end of the line.

Rebecca had scared the poor woman and felt terrible about that. This was a part of the job she hated. Talking to families to tell them their loved one was a suspect or criminal was second only to breaking the news about their death. This conversation was already an emotional roller coaster.

"Ma'am, you haven't been watching the news, have you?"

"Oh, God be merciful. No, I haven't. What's happened to my grandson?"

Pull the bandage off.

"He's taken several people hostage inside the Noble Lighthouse. He insists that his mother was killed. His actual words were, 'she was taken by the trees.' Do you know anything about that or why he would believe such things?"

"Oh, that poor boy." Lucy's voice was strained, sadness constricting her words. She cleared her throat. "He never believed his mother left him, and to be honest, I never thought my daughter would willingly abandon her son. She loved him so much. He was her world."

"Ma'am, I'm not criticizing, but it sounds like you didn't even know Mason left the group home."

"No, I wasn't aware. His father, that snake who my daughter married, made sure I couldn't visit him in the hospital or get any updates. Since my daughter went missing, he's done his best to keep me out of everything." Lucy blew her nose.

"Are you talking about Maria or Mason?"

"Both. I'm not even certain which day Maria went missing. I didn't know she was missing until I spoke with Mason. He was the one who told me he hadn't seen his mama in weeks. That she'd gone into the woods and didn't come back."

"And that's when you called the police?"

"Yes, ma'am. I spoke with a sheriff…oh, what was his name? Waldo?"

Rebecca bit back a laugh. Picturing the old sheriff as a

Waldo tickled her tired mind. "Do you mean Sheriff Wallace?"

"Yes, that's him. He did a wellness check. That was when Dennis finally admitted his wife had left him, taking only a few things. There wasn't even a note."

"Do you know why he didn't call the police?"

Lucy *tsked* sharply. "He said they'd argued over the boy, and she couldn't take it anymore and ran off. He didn't want anyone to think ill of his wife and hoped she would return once she'd had some time. I never bought that."

"And she'd never done anything like that before? Run off, I mean?"

"She did run off once over a summer between her junior and senior years in high school. Oh heavens, we turned the area upside down. Couldn't find her for almost two months. Turns out she was living with an older boyfriend she didn't want us to know about in some crappy apartment on the mainland."

Lucy's voice broke before continuing. "That was the only time she'd shown a defiant streak. And she adored Mason. No way she'd have left her own son. None. She was devoted to him. But I suspect her previous disappearance skewed the search, maybe got folks thinking Maria had run off again."

"What do you think was Dennis's reason for not notifying the authorities?"

"I think it was because that man cares about nothing but appearances. And he couldn't stand the world knowing he wasn't good enough for my daughter. As if everyone who met him a few times couldn't tell that for themselves." Lucy sighed. "Not in public, mind you. He does an excellent job of masking himself. He's like a chameleon. Fits in with anyone he's around, and you don't even know he's a reptile 'til you watch him when he doesn't know you're there. That happened early on when they were dating, and again when I was at the house, with Mason in his room."

That sounded an awful lot like a man she'd just recently met. Dennis Alton and Jeff Benton could be cut from the same cloth.

"Have you ever heard of a company called Coastal Properties?"

Lucy scoffed. "Those are the snakes that helped Dennis sell my family property. He sold my grandson's inheritance. Maria refused to sell to them because she knew the worth of the land. But Dennis never cared about that. He just wanted the big check they kept waving in his face. I guess he got it in the end."

It was Mason's inheritance? From his mother?

Rebecca would have to look into that and check for a will left by Maria. If Mason was supposed to inherit the property, Alton would have needed Mason's approval to sell it. And if that was the case, and he'd gotten Mason's blessing, then why was the young man so confused about his house not being where he remembered it?

Unless Alton had been able to prove Mason wasn't competent and the need was immediate. Then he could have gotten power of attorney to oversee Mason's inheritance. *That might not be a hard push with a judge when it's for a child who's been institutionalized with mounting medical expenses.*

"What was the market value of the property?"

"Well, aside from the seaside location, the trees."

"The trees?"

Why do the trees keep coming up?

"My ancestors planted bald cypress there. Even today, that lumber is worth a pretty penny. It's needed to make piers and whatnot. No matter what happened in Maria's life, she knew she could always count on the trees to keep her financially stable. Dennis never got that. He didn't want a modest source of reliable income. All he wanted was a big payday as soon as possible. He was never good at long-term planning but could snatch an opportunity out of thin air. That's how he caught Maria."

"How much were the trees worth?" If Jeff was as underhanded as Rebecca suspected, and Alton seemed indifferent to the homestead's value, she guessed that a simple review of the property sale record would show Alton was undercompensated for the land's true value.

"They provided my family a solid living. We'd sell the trees as needed, nothing regular. Sometimes we'd only need to sell off a large branch or fallen limbs. They grow very slowly, which makes the highly sought-after wood difficult to source. And since the wood has a wide variety of uses, it's really quite valuable. So long as the trees were cared for and properly harvested, they would always provide income. It was why I gave it to Maria early, so she wouldn't be financially dependent on that wretched man and could leave him if she wanted. I made sure to have it written up so that only my daughter and her children could own the property. But I guess Dennis managed to find a loophole."

The trees took her. Why would Mason say that if the trees were his true legacy? And why was he focusing so much on the lighthouse instead of the property where he lived?

"Actually, ma'am, he seems to be just as focused on the lighthouse being his fam...*your* family's legacy."

"Well, that's silly."

Rebecca knew then it would be a bad idea to have the woman come down. Telling Mason he was being silly wouldn't help matters.

"The only legacy we have on that property is the trees. We planted the same trees there as we did on the homestead."

Rebecca wasn't an arborist, but she had noticed that the trees surrounding the lighthouse were, in fact, cypress. With Mason's family homesite so close to the lighthouse, could he have been searching for the one place his family's trees remained? Perhaps the trees plus the name of the lighthouse had drawn him here.

"Thank you, ma'am. If we get any further updates, we'll call to let you know."

Rebecca gave Lucy Noble her contact information and ended the call as her heart clenched in pain.

"Please do, dear. I'd head on over, but I don't travel beyond the city limits without a driver."

There was so much intertwined in this case. Hostage situations were always complicated, but this wasn't what it appeared on the surface, Rebecca knew.

Benji and Hoyt were still laughing and talking, probably at her expense. Benji had been right beside her as they worked their way up the ranks of the FBI, so he'd gotten a front-row seat to all her blunders. Hopefully, the man remembered that she had seen his, as well, and refrained from sharing the truly embarrassing stories.

The lull provided the perfect chance to sit in the cruiser and do a quick search for missing persons cases in the cities Jeff Benton had listed. There were a lot of them. Too many for her to go through. Instead, she just flipped through the names. One of them caught her attention when she saw the last name.

Jo-Ellen Jean Gossard.

Jay Gossard? Didn't Mason stumble on that name? Maybe he'd actually said J.J. Gossard? Is it possible he meant Jo-Ellen Jean?

She opened the case file and started reading. Jo-Ellen Jean Gossard, also known as J.J., went missing from Virginia Beach after leaving a bar one night five years ago. She'd been a longtime resident of Virginia Beach but had no living relatives. It was her boss who reported her missing.

Unfortunately, that was all that was in the missing persons report. But Rebecca's skin was prickling, telling her she needed to dig deeper.

And that was exactly what Rebecca would do until she'd unearthed the truth.

25

As Rebecca stepped out of the cruiser, both Hoyt and Benji glanced over. Rebecca tipped her head up and raised her eyebrows. Both men nodded and followed her to where Dennis Alton stood.

Honestly, Rebecca was surprised the man had returned. He'd seemed so eager to leave yesterday, she couldn't imagine why he'd come back. Her gut told her it had nothing to do with concern for his son. By his own admission, he'd only bothered to visit his son a few times while he was institutionalized. So why even be here now? Of course, it wasn't like he was pestering her or the deputies for updates. Every time she'd seen him, he'd been on his phone.

"Mr. Alton, could we have a word with you?"

Alton looked up from his screen, locking it and dropping the device into his pocket.

Yeah, that's not suspicious at all.

"What can I do for you?"

"Special Agent Benji Huang." Benji flashed his credentials, and even though he was standing behind her, she knew he would be wearing his stone facade that had freaked out so many suspects before.

"Special...agent." Alton nodded and locked his gaze on Rebecca, clearly thinking she was the least scary of the bunch.

She was happy to dissuade him of that idea. "When Maria went missing, did you reach out to extended family? Did you ever check with them to see if she was staying there?"

"Yes, of course. As I told Sheriff Wallace at the time, none of them had heard from her."

"But you didn't reach out to Maria's mother, Lucy Noble." Benji wasn't the only one who could freak out liars with a flat tone and rocky expression.

"I...of course, I did. Lucy was my first call."

"Not according to Mrs. Noble. I just got off the phone with her. She says that not only did you *not* call her, you never answered when she called. You also blocked her from contacting Mason while he was getting help. Why was that?"

Alton scratched the end of his nose. *To keep it from growing?*

"Well, uhm, because, you see, he was quite upset about his mother. The doctors and I both thought having contact with his mother's mother would be detrimental to his health. You've seen his obsession with his maternal legacy." He tried to laugh, but it fell away when none of them responded favorably.

"That's the first time you've mentioned he was like this as a child too. If he was so obsessed with his legacy, then why did you sell it out from under him?"

He blinked. "What?"

"Why did you sell his inheritance, which he got from his *Noble* family line?" Rebecca stressed the name, making it sound more like an adjective instead.

Alton flapped his arms. "Well, I had to, didn't I? I'm sure

you don't know anything about it, having such great insurance through the government, but medical care is expensive in this country for the Average Joe. Do you think Mason's care was cheap? Hard times call for hard decisions, and I had to make them."

His answer was so smooth, Rebecca was certain he'd practiced it more than a few times. This man could've been a politician with the way he managed to not directly answer her questions. Or he would've made a great car salesman.

Beside her, Hoyt yawned. When Dennis Alton didn't, he nudged her arm.

Rebecca didn't allow herself to be sidetracked. "When Jeff Benton offered you that big check, you didn't have any other choice but to accept it, did you?"

"I didn't." Alton lifted his chin. "I'd already moved to the mainland into a small apartment. It was all I could afford. I was trying to make some extra money by renting out the old place. I did okay during peak season but didn't have the money to make the place fancy. That meant I didn't have many renters during the off season. Eventually, I had to sell the land. My last connection to my missing wife," he snapped his fingers, "gone, so I could keep my son healthy."

"How much did your son's medical expenses cost?"

Alton's mouth opened and closed like a trout. "I-I'm not sure, but it was very expensive over the years."

Unless it's on the government's dime.

Rebecca nodded. "Thank you, Mr. Alton. I'll be back when I have more questions."

She turned and walked off, Benji and Hoyt flanking her.

"What was all that about?" Hoyt asked.

"Jeff Benton and a timeline that doesn't work."

She quickly explained to both men the conversation she'd had with Lucy while searching for Agent Hazzard.

Once the brain trust was assembled, Rebecca explained

the discrepancies she was wrestling with. "Dennis claims he sold the Noble homestead to pay for Mason's expensive care."

Hoyt chewed his lip. "You mean the institution? Wasn't that government regulated?"

Benji interjected. "And a lot of those group homes are covered by insurance or the state too."

Rebecca nodded. "But don't long-term care homes require collateral? If the state had laid claim to the Alton property, Dennis wouldn't have been able to sell. And since he claims to have rented it out, could he even do that if the state had control of it?"

She made a note to see how Mason's care had been secured.

Benji's jaw tightened. "True. Lots of nursing care facilities now own their deceased patients' properties because of that very rule."

Rebecca's gut roiled. "Unless the patient was declared a threat to themselves or others." She glanced at Hoyt. "We need that warrant for Mason's hospital files, and we need to go through Mason's juvenile record more closely."

Hoyt hung his head. "I'm not sure everything that happened with that boy will be in his records. Wallace took care of that."

Rebecca sighed. The late sheriff seemed to be a good man on the surface, but he sure did hide a lot.

"Let's look anyway. If there was enough for Dennis Alton to have Mason committed for legal reasons, the state would pay that tab." She turned to stare at the father, whose nose was in his phone again. "Then all he had to do was wait until Maria was declared legally dead to sell."

Hoyt cursed. "And pocket all the money himself."

Rebecca touched her former partner's arm. "Benji, can you—"

He was already tapping on his phone. "Yeah. I'll access those files."

"What do you want me to do, Boss?" Hoyt asked.

"I want you to write down everything you remember about Mason. The types of calls you responded to. The results. The dates, as best as you can. We don't have time to dig through Wallace's pile of paper files on the chance that any of those calls were ones he kept off the books. After you've done that, give Viviane a call and cross reference your list against any files she's able to pull up. Ask her if she can pull up old rental listings to see how much income Dennis was making when he'd rent out the old home."

As if her words had conjured him, Mason started screaming. They all turned to look at the lighthouse.

Rebecca's heart squeezed. "As unlikely as it looks right now, I don't think our madman is as mad as he seems."

26

"You're right. Our boy is an early riser." Mason's garbled ramblings had begun a few minutes ago, and everyone had reconvened to see if he was willing to have a conversation.

Rebecca clutched her coffee cup and mulled over Agent Hazzard's assessment. "Yeah. Poor kid. If we're lucky, he'll ask for breakfast. Maybe we can get some negotiations started then."

Hazzard grunted but seemed focused on Mason's words.

And to be fair, it was dire. There were lots of mentions of choking, not breathing, and how it was all their fault. Everything he was yelling was so fast and convoluted that it didn't make much sense.

The negotiator had previously set sunrise as the deadline for Mason to surrender or SWAT would force its way inside. But with new information continuing to trickle in, Mason was looking less like a lunatic and more like a pawn. Even so, Mason's ramblings indicated they may have waited too long.

Finally, Mason paused long enough for Hazzard to respond. "Okay, Mason, slow down. I can't understand what you're talking about. Let's start with the basics. Who is choking?"

"The lady who wanted the oxygen yesterday. Nora. She's not waking up, and she's hardly breathing. The other old lady says she's going to die if you don't do something."

Rebecca tensed. "Tell him she can't save the lighthouse if she dies."

Hazzard nodded and triggered the mic. "Mason, this is serious. If that lady dies, she won't be able to save your lighthouse. Let us send in some medics to take care of her."

"No!" Mason shouted, sending the speaker into a staticky mess. "My mother died because I was helpless. I'm not helpless this time."

For a moment that sounded positive, like he might save Nora Weever.

"But *you* are! You're helpless. Just like I felt when my mom went away. I tried to tell you what happened to her, and no one listened. You all thought I was nuts. You still do. So the penalty for not listening is that this lady meets the same end as my mom. Unless you promise that no one is going to bulldoze my leg-a-see, this lady's gonna die in here. Do you want her to die? Admit to everyone out there that you don't care about this woman any more than you cared about my mom!"

"Give the EMTs a heads-up," Hazzard directed his team. "And tell everyone else to quietly get ready too. We're not going to wait for that woman to die."

There was no other way at this point. Rebecca couldn't even argue the case. They'd waited for nearly twenty-four hours already due to the twisted circumstances. Rebecca sighed and turned around to take a moment and just stare out at the wondrous view.

"The trees," she whispered.

Hoyt turned to her. "What did you say, Boss?"

Her mind raced as she took in the cypresses. "He said the

trees took his mom. Lucy said her family planted the trees. Not just the ones at their homestead, but here too. What if he didn't mean the trees at his house?"

Rebecca took a few steps, paused, crouched down slightly, then took a few more steps, trying to make the dots connect.

"What are you looking for?"

"Mason was a child back then, but the trees were shorter too. The Alton house is that way, right?"

Hoyt nodded. "As the crow flies, it's in that direction."

Rebecca walked that way. As she got close to the edge, she could see the SWAT team and the snipers waiting for their orders. Behind them, the old Alton Place had been replaced by construction crews and their equipment.

"The trees took her."

Benji stepped up next to her. "Ya know, Rebecca, maybe you should go ahead and take a vacation. You're starting to sound an awful lot like the crazy guy locked in the lighthouse."

"Not a crazy guy. A child. You know, kids tell us things that they perceive, not the way they literally happened, which can seem fantastical at the time. He wasn't even ten when his mother went missing. Learning all about the family land, and what made it so special. That the trees were his family legacy and even the lighthouse was named after their family."

Benji put a hand on her shoulder. "What are you talking about?"

Rebecca remembered he hadn't spoken to Dr. Montgomery. "His psychiatrist told us that, in some ways, Mason is still a child. He didn't finish maturing while in the institution. That's why he was in a group home afterward. She told us that Mason didn't need the meds the doctor at the institution, Dinton, had put him on, so she discontinued those when he went to the group home. Mason counted the days to his twentieth birthday and the release that came with that."

Benji rubbed his eye. "Okay, so if a kid, a ten-year-old, told me that the trees took his mother after she went missing and wasn't seen for years, I'd think someone dragged her into the woods and killed her."

"Exactly. I need to talk to Mason." Rebecca spun on her heel, calling over her shoulder. "Would you tell Hazzard to hold off on storming the castle? I might have a way to end this peacefully."

"Boss!" Hoyt called, but she waved him off and kept walking toward the lighthouse door.

Please don't let me be wrong.

"Mason!" She knocked on the door. "It's Sheriff West again. I need to talk to you."

"What do you want?" Mason was close, just on the other side of the wood.

"Nora can't help you. She didn't know anything about the lighthouse being taken down. She also can't help you figure out what happened."

"Then what good is she?"

Rebecca blew out a long breath. "Nora Weever can't help you. But I can. Let her go and I'll take her place."

27

"Back away. I need time to think." Mason's voice shook with confusion.

Rebecca backed away, stopping about fifteen feet from the door. Far enough away to react if anything happened and still be able to talk to her team, if she needed, without being overheard.

"Sheriff West, that's not something I can allow to happen." Agent Hazzard's voice came over her radio. "And quite frankly, ma'am, what the hell do you think you're doing?"

All eyes were on Rebecca, and not all of them came from the line of uniformed officers behind her. Mason was watching her. She was sure of it. She hoped the snipers would stand down even if Mason presented a clear target.

She triggered her mic. "I'm getting a dying woman out of there, and I believe I can end this peacefully. I think I finally figured out what Mason has been trying to say this whole time."

"Putting another person in danger is not how we do things," Hoyt broke in.

"Lordy, Rebecca, you're not doing what I think you're

doing." Viviane's shaking voice came over the radio. "Are you?"

Rebecca sighed. "I am. Seriously, he hasn't made a single violent move since he first got here."

"You mean other than the little old lady he shot?" Darian's voice was filled with sarcasm.

Rebecca ignored them all. "Besides, he's just one man. If I get the chance, I can take him down, and we can end this quickly. All I need to do is disable him long enough for everyone to get out. We're closing in on twenty-four hours already."

"Okay, she does have a point there."

It was good to know Darian at least supported her. Because she was going forward regardless. There was a long silence, and she knew her men were talking with the SWAT team and Hazzard about her.

"Sheriff West, I, as the crisis negotiator, cannot condone or approve of your actions." Hazzard's tone was flat as a still pond and carried no hint of emotion.

"I hear you, Agent Hazzard." And she did, every word he *wasn't* saying. If she did this and things went bad, it was her ass on the line. But she was used to that by now. "I'm doing this of my own volition and against all advice and standard operating procedure."

She blew out a deep breath, trying to ignore the memories of the last time she'd—

"Rebecca, don't make this like last time." Benji had moved to where she barely had to turn her head to see him.

The smell of blood mixed with oil.

Headlights bobbing.

A dying man screaming.

Her shoulder pulsating with pain.

"Sheriff West!"

Rebecca forced her attention back on the door and the young man behind it. "I'm still here, Mason."

"I'll make the trade."

Ice raced through Rebecca's veins, but she started walking before her body could refuse. "I'm coming in now."

"No. Wait! First, I want you to handcuff your hands together, so you can't hurt me."

Shit.

The kid had some street smarts. Rebecca bet he was smarter than most people gave him credit for.

"If I handcuff myself, how can I get Nora out the door?" She mentally crossed her fingers that the excuse would fly.

"I got people to do that. Gracie and Bob are going to put her outside. Once you're all back inside, then the ambulance people can come get her."

Ambulance people. Smart, but still a child.

"Deal."

Before he had to ask, Rebecca unbuckled her duty belt and let it fall to the ground. She tucked the tiny pouch that held the key to her cuffs inside her waistband. Then, making sure Mason could see her actions, she pulled her handcuffs free, wrapped them around her wrists in front of her body, and snapped them closed.

Other than that, she also had her phone in her pocket. This was the best she could hope for. Better than a gun, better than handcuffs, a cop's real main weapon should always be their mind.

"Sheriff West, this is Dr. Montgomery. Agent Hazzard wanted me to give you my opinion on this. Mason is unstable, but I truly do not believe he would choose to hurt someone. He might lash out and people could end up in harm's way, but he does not aim to cause harm."

The metal around Rebecca's wrists clinked when she triggered her mic. "Good to know at least one professional thinks the way I do."

"The rest of us think you're nuts."

She smiled. "Yeah, well, for that, Greg, tell Locke to free Chad Weever from the interrogation room, so he can go see his mother at the hospital."

"Yeah, Boss. Watch your back."

The door pushed open, and an elderly man and woman struggled to hold a second elderly lady. All three of them were smeared with dried blood.

"Set her to the side," Mason ordered. "Hurry up."

Rebecca couldn't see the young man, but she definitely saw the gun pointed at the hostages. For a man who seemed so gullible and inexperienced, Mason had been alarmingly adept at keeping trained snipers at bay. Or perhaps it was because he was so childlike that this incident had dragged on as long as it had.

"You're gonna be okay now, Nora. You made it out. Just keep breathing. Okay. Keep breathing." Tears trickled down Gracie William's cheeks. Rebecca recognized her from her driver's license photo. The other volunteer appeared to be Bob Dolan. They set Nora Weever down on the ground and propped her up against the side of the lighthouse.

"Now, you three come inside and the ambulance people can come get her."

When Rebecca stepped inside, she took in her surroundings. Two of the hostages returned to the far side of the lighthouse's interior to sit down beside the third hostage, who must've been Chuck Anderson. Cardboard boxes had been torn open, with piles of sweatshirts and other clothing turned into makeshift bedding.

Although the median age of the hostages was close to seventy-seven, a fun fact Darian Hudson had shared with

Rebecca over a lukewarm cup of coffee, Mason still trained his gun on the group.

"Shut the door." Mason waved the gun at Rebecca. "You, you stay right there. If they start shooting, you'll be a good target."

With one more glance at the outside world, Rebecca pulled the door closed.

Mason grinned when she turned to face him. "Now we can make sure the trees don't take anyone else."

28

For the first two hours, Hoyt stood on pins and needles as they listened to Rebecca casually narrate her surroundings.

So far, she'd confirmed who the three other hostages were besides Rebecca. There was food and water inside, which explained why the food truck hadn't been as tempting as they'd hoped. The hostages were using a bucket for a bathroom. And, most importantly, they learned from Rebecca's hushed conversations with the hostages that Mason hadn't slept since entering the lighthouse. He'd told everyone it was nighttime, and nobody could talk, but he hadn't closed his own eyes.

That worried the shit out of Hoyt, even though he'd suspected as much. A lone gunman could hardly fall asleep safely in this situation. But sleep deprivation on top of Mason's already compromised emotional state wasn't a good combination.

"What is she doing in there?"

Doctor Montgomery answered Hoyt's question without looking at him. "Considering how worked up Mason was when she went inside, I'm betting she's allowing him time to calm down. That's very smart of her."

"Well, I don't like it."

"Then how about I give you something to do." The question sounded more like a statement as Benji Huang walked up holding three pieces of paper. "Rebecca asked me to look up those dates. You'll want to see this."

Hoyt took the papers. "The property sales info?"

"Dennis Alton got his son's property handed over to him. That judge has since been let go for judicial misconduct. I haven't dug up the why of that yet, but I will. Also, the day after Maria Alton was declared dead, Dennis Alton sold the family home and acreage to Coastal Properties. After surveys, permits, and architectural plans were acquired, they broke ground two years later."

"So he was just waiting for that declaration of death." Hoyt sighed heavily and shook his head. This was what he was afraid of. They missed something in their investigation back then. But then again, they hadn't even been notified of Maria going missing for two weeks. That was a long time for a trail to go cold.

"That's not a coincidence." Benji tapped his middle finger along his leg. "Why does she always have to be like this?"

"Who? Sheriff West?"

"Yes. Rebecca always runs when she should walk. Always puts in a hundred percent when ninety will do. Trusts people she shouldn't."

Hoyt chuckled. "I haven't known her as long as you, but the West I know doesn't trust easy."

Benji snorted. "Well, at least she's learning."

"She also doesn't go rushing in without a good reason."

"A good reason to *her*." Benji shook his head. "She should hold back more often. Wait for situations to stabilize before charging in."

Hoyt waited to see if Benji would explain that any further, but he didn't. "That might work for the FBI, but that doesn't work out on the streets."

"That must be why she seems so much more comfortable around you guys than she ever did around us." Benji's tapping finger stilled. "That makes me happy. She was an excellent agent, but she didn't seem happy. Some people just don't fit into a tightly regulated job with so many supervisors."

"Now *that* sounds like my boss."

Darian walked up rubbing his hands together. "We swapping tales about the boss?"

"That depends." Hoyt lifted an eyebrow. "Did you come over because you have an update?"

"Yeah, another state vehicle pulled up. They said you called them in?"

"It's about damn time. Come on." Hoyt turned and headed for the road. Both men followed. "Once I realized what the sheriff was catching on to, I called up a buddy of mine. Rebecca shouldn't have to keep cleaning up after us because Wallace and I didn't do a thorough enough job to begin with."

Benji grabbed Hoyt's arm. "What are you talking about?"

Chastity Green lowered the van's window. "Hey, Hoyt, do you want us to set up here or somewhere else?"

Hoyt pointed toward the old Alton land. "I'm going to need you to start across the way. I'll send one of my men with you." He pointed at Darian, who raised his eyebrows but didn't say a word. "The sheriff is a bit caught up in things, so I'll be taking point on this."

Chastity chuckled. "No, you'll be taking rear. Daisy always takes point. And you don't want to argue with her."

"Yes, ma'am." Hoyt tipped his hat. "I know better than to interfere with a professional woman going about her job. But if she finds what I'm afraid she'll find, I'll buy her a box of biscuits."

A mixture of baying and barking rang out from the back of the van. Chastity waggled a finger at Hoyt. "You just had to say the B word, didn't you?"

He winced. "I didn't think. I'm sorry."

Chastity whistled over her shoulder and the barking stopped, but the baying of the hound only slowed. "Well, tell me where I'm going, so I can get them out of here before I go deaf." She wagged her finger again. "And you'd better come through with those B words too. Or my pack will go apeshit on you."

Darian lifted onto his tiptoes, attempting to see inside the van's window. "You called in search and rescue dogs?"

Hoyt wished. "Cadaver."

"Best in the area." The woman beamed and held her hand out. "I'm Chastity Green. That's my husband, Abe."

Abe waved from the passenger seat.

"Pleased to meet you, ma'am." Darian shook her hand but looked confused. "Who are we looking for?"

Hoyt held up a finger. The Greens had arrived sooner than he thought they would. He had some explaining to do.

"Give me a minute. I need to clear this with SWAT and the hostage negotiator, so they know you're coming."

Triggering his mic, he communicated this new development to the team. "One of my deputies will accompany them to the old Alton Place."

After receiving confirmation, Hoyt turned to Darian. "Escort them to the area. We don't have a warrant, but I don't think the foreman of the job site will mind a couple of dogs moseying around." He jotted the names down on his notepad and ripped the paper off. "If he doesn't give permission, let me know."

Darian took it. "Will all that construction mess up their noses?"

Chastity chuckled. "My pack can find a body that's been dead between an hour and forever. Doesn't matter what else is there. So long as that body is still decomposing, they'll find it."

"I'll lead the way." Darian jogged off to his cruiser. A few seconds later, the van followed.

Eager to see if he'd missed anything happening inside the lighthouse, Hoyt searched for Benji, who'd wandered off. He scanned the area.

Dr. Montgomery, Brenda Langley, Agent Hazzard... Huh, looks like Alton *left. Mason's doctor and babysitter are still standing here worried, but not his dad. Interesting.*

And where was Benji?

Someone saying the sheriff's full name caught his attention and he turned to a crowd of onlookers. Benji was standing just on the inside of the tape, chatting with the reporter from Richmond.

Anger and disappointment hit Hoyt like a brick, and he walked over to the two men.

"What exactly do you think you're doing?"

Oscar Toullaine didn't bother to even look his way, let alone have the manners to look guilty. "I'm just getting some background for Sheriff West's story. Finding her old partner here was too good to pass up."

Hoyt ignored Oscar, who was still holding a recording device up to Benji's mouth.

He pulled Benji back a few steps. "Does the sheriff know you're doing this?"

The agent shrugged. "I'm not telling him anything Rebecca wouldn't want them to know. Just about being her partner and her qualifications. That's information anyone can access."

"Then let him access it somewhere else. I may not have known her as long as you, but around here, we consider it rude to talk about people behind their backs. Especially to the press."

Benji led him even farther away from the reporter. "Deputy, I love how much loyalty Rebecca inspires in her people. The reporter assured me that's the angle he wants to take with his article. He isn't looking for dirt on Rebecca. He stated it would be an uplifting story, not a hit piece."

Hoyt wasn't sure if he believed that. "Well, that's all well and good, but this is still an active crime scene, and I need to get back to my job." With a final assessing glare at the agent, Hoyt turned and strode back to his SUV.

The gravel shifted behind him as Benji followed. "I didn't see any harm in giving him what he wants and keeping him distracted. I've found that if you humor the press every now and then, they stay out of your hair. Look behind me. Is that guy still standing there?"

Hoyt glanced back. "Nope, he's gone."

"Because I gave him enough to placate his editor, and his main target is out of reach. Now he has what I gave him, not some bits he overheard that he tries to piece together."

That did sound like a better outcome, and Hoyt's unease settled a bit.

The special agent held his gaze. "Rebecca is my friend. That's why I came down. I'm looking out for her like I have since we met at Quantico. She's my partner, even if we don't work for the same agency anymore. I'm not about to let the press sully her name."

"That's good." Hoyt glanced at the lighthouse. "Because she's my partner now. And I'm watching her back too."

29

The king junior suite at the Tidepool Motel did not live up to its name. The bed was a king, but it took up most of the room. The "suite" was split by a half wall with a microwave on top of a mini fridge on one side. It was the type of room I'd normally never be caught dead in.

I laughed at my unintentional joke, then froze as I heard a noise.

This place was so old, they still handed out keys on little plastic ovals with the room numbers on them. They made a distinctive sound as the key was put into the lock. Enough warning to let me know to get ready.

And I'm certainly ready.

Inside the bathroom, I slowed my breathing, tightening the lamp cord around my gloved fists.

Come on. Take a piss.

Instead, the bed creaked.

Okay. Plan B it was.

Peeking around the door, I spotted my target sitting on the side of the bed. His head was bent, his thumbs flying over the screen of his phone.

After a long inhale, I stepped through the doorway.

He never even saw me walk up to him.

Not until it was too late.

His head shot up, exposing his neck. Never one to miss such a golden opportunity, I lunged. It only took a second to wrap the cord around it and force him face-first onto the floor, my knee in his back. His busted nose spewed blood onto the ugly carpet.

He bucked me like a bull, and I pulled up with the cord. He flailed his arms, searching for a weapon. I pulled tighter, and his hands went to his throat, scratching at the garrote slowly killing him.

"It'll be better if you don't fight back. It'll be over faster." I leaned forward, putting all my weight on his spine.

"Why?" he managed to gasp.

"Sorry, but this is out of my hands. I'm just doing what needs to be done."

Pulling harder, I began to hum my favorite song, "Money" by Pink Floyd.

At just under five minutes long, the song was the perfect length to make sure the man beneath me was well and truly dead. Closing my eyes, I gave him privacy as he transitioned from this life into the next.

I wasn't a psychopath, after all. I didn't enjoy watching him suffer. It was just a means to an end.

Once the song was finished, I pushed to my feet and wiped the sweat from my forehead, careful not to let a single drop escape the towel.

Now I could get to work.

30

Rebecca was pleasantly surprised that the lighthouse stayed fairly cool even as the sun passed its peak. However, she wasn't happy that Mason didn't seem the least bit interested in talking with her. It'd been a few hours already. The movement of the sun over the circular glass dome made it easy to watch the time tick by. It was like living inside a sundial.

He'd been raving mad when she first got there, not saying anything useful and growing more aggravated each time she said his name. Now he was just mumbling to himself and pacing around, the gun jerking in different directions.

Rebecca had planted herself about ten feet away from where Gracie, Bob, and Chuck huddled on the sweatshirts serving as bedding. If she said anything that angered Mason, she wanted to be safely away from them.

Gracie rolled a bottle of water Rebecca's way. With a grateful smile, she took it but didn't open it just yet.

This was why Mason hadn't requested food or water. The Preservation Society had quite the little spread laid out on a table. A cooler sat beneath it.

"Mason, can we talk?"

Mason twisted around. "What? Why?"

She smiled, forcing a softness into her expression and tone. "Because we need to figure out what happened to your mom. Right?" She leaned forward slightly. "Can you do that? Can you remember what happened the night the trees took your mom?"

He lurched forward a few steps, the gun swinging wildly. "Yes. I remember every minute of it. The way the trees rushed up around."

Rebecca held her cuffed hands up, palms out. "What was she doing before the trees took her?"

"It was family night. We were playing games. It was Monopoly. I remember it so well." He smiled, and his eyes focused on something just over her head. "I was beating my dad for a change. He was mad. So mad, he had to go for a walk. Ma went after him. We never finished the game."

"What happened next?"

"And then…nothing. The trees took Ma." Mason looked away, shuffling his feet.

"Mason, I don't understand. Are you telling me the truth?"

"I'm not lying!" He stomped his foot.

Rebecca patted the air in a placating manner. "I'm not saying you're lying. But I do need you to tell me *all* the truth. I talked with your babysitter. And some other people who know you. They told me you were rambunctious back then. You were always sneaking out of the house and running around."

He ducked his head, looking like that rambunctious child he had once been. "Okay."

"If your mom and dad left, then how did you see the trees take your mother?"

Mason mumbled something.

"What was that?"

"I snuck out." Guilt dripped from his words.

From the corner of her eye, Rebecca watched Gracie, Chuck, and Bob's expressions morph from angry to scared. It was disturbing to witness a grown man, even a young one, acting like a troubled child.

Rebecca would have to treat him as one to relate to him. "Of course you did. You love your mom. And she was concerned for your dad. It makes sense that you followed them. Also, I bet you were really looking forward to showing your dad how smart and grown-up you were, right?"

Mason smiled, but it faded quickly. "He hated that."

"That you were growing up?"

"No. That I was better than him at something. He said it was only because of luck. I laughed and said I was luckier than him."

"I bet he didn't like that."

"He didn't. That's why he got angry. Then he got loud. Ma said he was just angry because things were tight."

"Tight?"

Mason shook his head. "She never told me what was tight. Then she went to talk to Dad outside. After that, it got louder, even though they weren't in the house. I tried not to hear what they were saying."

"What were you doing while they were talking?"

He brought his fists up to his ears. "I did this when it got loud."

Rebecca didn't like the picture Mason was painting. The sheriff had been called out for yelling and screaming, disturbing the peace. They blamed the son because he was so rambunctious. What if none of those calls were for Mason being loud? What if Mason was just their scapegoat?

"But you could still see them? Where were you?"

"In the kitchen."

"Could you see out the kitchen window?"

"Yes."

"And what did you see? Was it dark?"

"Kinda dark. That blue dark that happens before the real dark."

"Twilight?" The more Mason spoke, the more he seemed to regress in time along with his childhood memories. But at least they were getting all of this recorded on the microphone at the door.

"Yeah. Ma ran off into the trees. Dad followed after."

Rebecca waited for him to finish, but he didn't.

"What happened after that?" she prodded.

"I saw Ma. Through the trees. Barely. It was hard to see, and that's when I went outside, but I was very quiet. She fell down and didn't get up again. I ran back inside. And then they were both gone. Dad came back later."

"Did he say anything?"

"He said that Ma was with those damn trees she loved so much. They took her away from him because she refused to give up on them." Mason frowned, his eyebrows dipping together. "Then he went into their office and didn't come out for a long time. But he got loud in there too. When he came out, I asked him when Ma was coming home."

"And what did your dad say?"

Mason hit his head with his fist.

"Mason? When did your dad say your mom would come back?"

"Never ever. The trees took her." Tears rolled down his cheeks. "You know, the same thing happened to Paddy and J.J. They disappeared."

And that brought Rebecca around to the unused puzzle pieces.

Mason blinked to clear the tears. "I heard about them, and then I went to the VCIN, that's the—"

"Virginia Criminal Information Network." Rebecca knew her hunch was right and that there was more to Mason than most people saw. She just had to get him talking about something in his wheelhouse. His love of crime videos, solving his mom's disappearance…this had become his whole world over the last decade.

"Please, continue, Mason. I didn't mean to interrupt you."

"So my mom was in the database. And I checked it every day. I don't know why, I just did. Then, after I heard about Paddy and J.J., I checked, and they were there too."

"I understand. Keep going." He was on a roll, and Rebecca didn't want him to stop.

"That's it. The trees took them too. That's what I keep telling everyone!"

Rebecca didn't want to rile him up, but she needed just a little bit more to decode his message. "Mason, who told you that the trees took Paddy and J.J.?"

Mason looked down at his shoes and started fidgeting with his gun. She was getting somewhere. If she asked him enough easy questions, she knew he'd inadvertently answer the one she needed answered most. This was a basic tactic of interrogation.

"Mason, what are Paddy and J.J.'s real names?"

"I don't remember. I'm sorry."

"Well, how can I find out?"

"My dad might—"

His eyes got big, like a child who just got caught drawing with a crayon on the walls.

"It's okay, Mason. If we want to save the lighthouse, everything you tell us will help. It's really okay. Your dad wants us to help you. He'd want you to tell us everything you know."

"Dad and the sheriff went out looking for Ma a couple of

times, you know. I even went with them the first night." He started pacing.

Mason was protecting his father, his only other parent. It made sense to Rebecca.

"But we never found her. I told them about the trees, but no one believed me. No one believed me. No one would listen!"

And he was gone again.

But the big question on Rebecca's mind was, had this mentally unstable man-child with a deadly weapon and a crop of hostages just assisted the authorities in solving three missing persons cases?

31

"I believe you." Rebecca's tone was soft and comforting, barely louder than a whisper.

Everyone in the lighthouse froze. Even Mason.

Bob stared at her. "You do?"

"About his mom, at least." She settled her gaze on Mason. "I believe you about what happened to your mom. What I still don't understand is why you brought a gun here and decided to hold these people hostage."

Rebecca's phone chimed.

Mason lifted the gun. "What's that?"

"It's my phone." It was tough for Rebecca to maneuver with the handcuffs on, but she managed to pull the device from her pocket. "I told you I believed you. So before I came in here, I had my men investigating. Between what we already knew and what you told us, we were able to put some things together. Did you hear those dogs barking?"

He nodded. "Yeah."

"Do you know what that means?" She didn't give him time to answer. "It means we started a new search."

She didn't know that for sure, but she'd bet her next paycheck on it.

"Don't lie to me. You searched before and didn't find her."

"You're right. I just don't think they looked hard enough."

Mason sank to the floor, his knees finally giving out. "They didn't. They yelled her name a million times, but they should have yelled a million and one."

Rebecca's heart squeezed. "Mason, do you know what cadaver dogs are?"

Considering how many unsolved-crime shows he'd clearly watched, she was confident he would be familiar with them.

He swallowed hard. "Those are the dogs that find dead bodies. They sniff them out anywhere, no matter how long they're dead."

Rebecca held up her phone, showing him the messages.

"You already know Deputy Hoyt Frost. Here, Hoyt is letting me know the dogs arrived on your family's property. And below that, Darian is telling me they've finished searching the land around your old house and are heading this way. If we stay quiet, we can probably hear the dogs barking in the trees, looking for your mother."

Mason eyed her suspiciously but shifted closer to look at her screen.

"I heard dogs earlier."

She nodded. "Exactly." She tapped on a picture showing a dog in front of the luxury condo sign. "You can see for yourself."

"Why didn't they do that before? She'd been gone for two whole weeks. Those dogs can find people when they've only been missing for a—"

"Sheriff Wallace didn't know, and there was evidence that made him believe she'd run away." Rebecca gentled her voice even more. "Mason, do you understand why we have cadaver dogs out there today?"

Mason dipped his head, tears brimming in his eyes. "Because you're looking for my mom's dead body."

32

Darian loved watching the dogs work.

He'd been thinking about becoming a K-9 handler, and watching Chastity and Abe handle their dogs was a reminder to talk to the sheriff about getting him the classes.

He grinned as the dogs worked, in awe of their total focus. When he watched Daisy step over the bones of what looked to be a squirrel, Darian shook his head in wonder.

"How can they tell human and animal remains apart?" he asked Chastity.

"Training." She glanced at him and smiled at his obvious disappointment. "It's a simple answer that actually involves hundreds of dedicated hours of having the dog focus only on the scent of human decay."

"Why did you choose cadavers for your specialty?"

Her smile faded. "Because everyone needs closure."

Another simple answer, but this one clearly contained the weight of grief.

"I'm sorry."

Chastity shrugged. "Thanks." One side of her mouth

tipped up. "Besides, it's better than training them to sniff out bedbugs."

Darian's mouth popped open. "Seriously? They train dogs for that?"

"Yep."

Don't let the bedbugs bite.

Darian's arms began to itch, and Chastity laughed. She stopped when Daisy sank to the ground.

"She's found something."

Darian jogged beside the trainer to where the dog lay. That was how Daisy communicated. She'd been allowed off leash with the command to "search." When she found something, she'd stay right where she was until her handler arrived.

"Good girl." Chastity marked the spot for forensics and gave Daisy her toy to play with as a reward.

"Deputy Hudson?" A state trooper in a crisp, fresh uniform was heading his way. She made sure to stay out of the cadaver dogs' search area as she approached.

"That's me. Can I help you with something?"

"I'm here to take over for you. You've got a visitor."

Darian looked around but didn't see anyone. "A visitor?"

"Viviane Darby? She's parked on the road over that way. We thought it would be the closest place to your location."

Darian pulled out his phone. He knew he hadn't missed anything on the radio, and he hadn't gotten a call or text either. The road wasn't visible from here beyond the foliage. Still, he knew where it was, and the trip was quick.

"Ya know, if you were wearing camo out there, I'd never have noticed you sneaking up on me, stomping through the trees like that." Viviane laughed from where she was leaning against her car.

"That's why I'm stomping instead of sneaking. Wouldn't want you getting scared. Having a woman scream in fright would not be a good idea, for my health or anyone else's sanity."

Viviane didn't wait for him to reach her and instead walked out to meet him. She handed him a bottle of water. "You're really out here looking for Maria Alton's body?"

Darian wiped the sweat from his forehead and dried his hand on his pants. "Yup, that's the theory. At least, so far."

"I knew them, ya know. Well, I suppose everyone knew them. Dennis was such a crap husband, no one doubted she'd left him. I was young then, twenty-something, but I'd heard my mother and her friends talk about it, about him. But the idea that she was killed, that's harder to believe. Have you found anything?"

Darian debated whether to tell her the truth or not. In the end, he determined that if she was asking the question, she was ready for the answer.

"The cadaver dogs marked one spot, but we're waiting for forensics to arrive. Chastity says that could be where someone was killed."

Viviane frowned, and he worried he'd made the wrong choice. "How could they tell if that was where someone died if they're cadaver dogs? Isn't it decomposition they're trained to smell?"

"Decomposing flesh in the soil. These dogs can find people who've been dead twenty-five years."

"Is it Maria's flesh?" Her voice was soft and pained, but he had to give her credit for asking anyway, even though it involved someone she knew.

"We're not sure if it's *hers*, just that it's human decay."

Violent nodded. "And you don't want to make assumptions that will bias the investigation moving forward."

Darian was impressed. "Exactly. Tunnel vision is the death of an investigation. And it could be the death of your coworkers too." He cleared his throat and looked around, even though he knew there was no one nearby. In the distance, they could vaguely hear the search party still moving through the woods, but there was no way anyone would hear them talking.

"I had an LT who was certain, dead certain, that we were on the track of hunting down an al-Qaeda cell dealing in information. He knew what it was, in his mind, and every piece of intel we got he made fit into that view of things."

Viviane nodded. "Confirmation bias?"

"Yeah. We walked right into an ambush. It wasn't even al-Qaeda. It was from a local arms dealer." He swallowed so hard his ears popped, and he could swear he still felt that damn sand stuck in his boots, despite the ocean sounds and smells around him. "We were pinned down for three days until we could get air support to scatter them."

The grit of the sand on his raw flesh gnawed at his mind, but he knew he couldn't move or the sniper would get him.

He blinked five times. Tapped his finger four times. Flexed his toes three times. Counted as he inhaled and exhaled, then nodded once, settling himself back in the here and now.

Memories belong in the past. They're real, but not here. I am.

Viviane squeezed his arm. "Are you okay?"

Darian smiled and knew it was shaky. "No, but I'm getting better." He blew out a harsh breath that was nearly a laugh. "That damn West. Damn her. She's working through her issues so soon after her shit hit the fan. It made me realize I need to do better about dealing with mine."

He almost blurted out how bad he felt about not joining his wife and baby girl on the beach, but that was a step too far for him. He could admit his disgust of sand to Rebecca or Hoyt. He shuddered as he remembered the feel of the grains slipping under his boots as he raced to provide Rebecca backup at the beach when she'd stumbled over that fresh body.

The blood on the sand, his CO crouching low for cover, the explosions in the air from the fireworks and the scent of gunpowder and sulfur in the air. The nightmares had started again and it fucking sucked.

Warm fingers touched Darian's arm, and his eyes snapped back into focus.

Viviane looked up at him, concern shining in her dark eyes. "Tell me about the case. What do we need to find? And if we do find a body, does that change how things will be handled with Mason and the hostages?"

He appreciated the change of topic. "Legally speaking, it probably won't." She frowned and he shrugged. "It might not be what you want to hear because you knew him as a kid, but come on, Viviane. He could've come to any of us at any time once he was free and told us what happened. We would've investigated just as thoroughly. Hell, we could've done a better job without the distractions to our resources and the stressful timeline."

"I know." Viviane twisted her earring. "And that's something I need to work on. I can be sympathetic to their problems, but I still need to see cases without the bias and stick to SOP and laws."

That seemed a bit strange to Darian. As their dispatcher, Viviane didn't have to worry about such things. In fact, she rarely, if ever, interacted with the suspects. She usually wasn't even on the scene, like she was now. Of course, she'd stopped by to drop off the rental income information Rebecca had asked her to obtain. But this felt different. Was it just her personal interest in the case? Or was there something more?

Darian was distracted when his radio popped to life.

"Deputy Hudson, we found something."

He leaned in and gave his friend and colleague a half hug. "Sorry. I've got to go."

As if his gesture of affection fueled her with a new resolve, Viviane straightened her shoulders and began walking. "Right. Let's go."

33

Mason had gone back to his pacing and mumbled ranting under his breath. He was also so focused on his own monologue that he didn't seem to notice when the hostages scooted closer to Rebecca.

"How's Nora?" Gracie asked, concern written in every line of her face.

Keeping an eye on Mason, Rebecca typed a message to Hoyt, asking for an update.

"I'll let you know as soon as I do."

Chuck Anderson wanted to know if his family had arrived. Apparently, his wife, two daughters, and five grandchildren had gone to Orlando for the week. Chuck shook his head. "I should've gone with them. Hard to believe I thought Disney would kill me."

"What are you all talking about?"

Gracie made a little yipping noise that made Rebecca smile. "Disney."

Mason frowned but didn't say anything more. He began pacing again, resuming his muttered monologue.

Bob Dolan leaned forward, voice low. "What's Vale got to do with this?"

Rebecca shrugged. "We're not sure yet." She changed the subject. "Tell me what happened when Mason first came in." She'd already asked them, but like any good detective, she'd ask the same question several times.

In hushed snippets, Chuck said he'd counted four shots.

Bob shook his head. "Three."

Gracie held up two fingers.

Still not helpful.

Knowing exactly how many bullets had been fired would have been useful. Mason's gun was a revolver. With a maximum capacity of six rounds, he might only have two bullets left. Or four. She wouldn't put her life, or the lives of the hostages, in danger based on often unreliable statements from witnesses.

Rebecca had also been fed details of Mason's initial rants. Evidence that a few boxes of souvenirs had been torn open and some of the logoed mugs smashed was clear even to an untrained eye.

Their captor's nonsensical diatribes chopping up the long bouts of silence and inaction kept the hostages subdued. He'd also been repeating stories about his mom and his lighthouse legacy.

No one knew what he would do. When they'd asked for water, he'd kicked the cooler and berated them for wanting to defile the landmark. But when a few of them had been desperate enough to ask for food on display on the table, they went ignored as Mason continued to talk about how important the lighthouse was.

Rebecca's phone rang again, and Mason turned the gun on her. The hostages, who'd been leaning toward her, jerked away.

Rebecca held up her hands, the phone in one palm to

show him who was calling. "This is why you have me in here, right? To get answers. They wouldn't have called unless they had something new."

"Answer it. But I want to hear too." Mason lowered the gun, tapping the barrel against his leg.

"This is Sheriff West. Hoyt, you're on speaker."

There were a few beats of silence before Hoyt responded. "Boss, I'm, uh, not sure how to say this now."

Shit. Shit. Shit.

Mason snatched the phone away from Rebecca. "Tell me the truth. Stop hiding things from me!"

"Mason," Hoyt's voice was soft and kind, not in the least bit anxious, "I regret to inform you that we found remains that appear to be your mother in an unmarked grave."

"I told you. The trees took her! She's in the trees because they took her from me. I saw it! But no one believed me until now." He sounded elated, vindicated even, as tears streamed down his cheeks. The gun clanked as he smacked it against his head.

Blood trickled down his temple.

Gracie gasped, pressing her fingertips over her lips. "Oh, honey, that's so terrible. I'm so sorry for you."

"So is it? Is it really my mother? Don't hide this from me. After all these years, I need to know." Mason scraped the cylinder of the gun against his scalp, his fingers white where they gripped Rebecca's phone hard.

Rising to her feet, Rebecca took half a step toward him, raising her cuffed hands to placate him. Wild eyes stared back at her. His gun wasn't pointing at anyone, but things could go wrong in a flash.

"Mason, remember the shows you used to watch? Did they ever tell you how bodies are identified after they've been buried?"

He nodded. "Through tests and…stuff. DNA?"

Rebecca tried to put it in terms Mason could understand. "That's right. And we can't do those tests while our evidence is in the ground. If we want to protect it, we have to be careful how we take it out. But you can help with the DNA tests." She paused until he met her gaze. "If you want."

"That's right, Mason," Hoyt said. "If you're willing to come with us and give us a sample of your DNA, we can get that test done to make sure it's your mother we found."

Rebecca monitored him for any hint of how he might react. This was a make-or-break moment.

Mason swallowed hard. "How can I know you're telling the truth? What if the body isn't hers at all?"

"That's a very good question and the answer is painful." Hoyt paused, as if pondering how much to reveal. "The body is wearing a necklace."

Mason's body went rigid, and his eyes unfocused, concerning Rebecca. *Was he having a medical emergency?* The others shifted uncomfortably. She'd been in here with his chaotic actions for several hours. How bad it must be for the others who'd endured it for more than twenty-four hours already.

"The necklace has a name on it. It reads Noble."

"That's my mom's necklace. I got it for her for Mother's Day. Gramma helped me get it. She loved it and always wore it."

A sob broke out behind her, and Rebecca turned to see Bob holding a weeping Gracie.

"Will you help us identify the body, Mason?" Rebecca asked him softly.

He shook his head and looked around. "Ma is gone. I need to protect the lighthouse. I'm the keeper now."

Rebecca wasn't sure he was seeing what everyone else could see.

"This is where it gets tricky."

She nearly groaned when Hoyt said that and wished she had the phone in her hand so she could hang up before he said anything else.

Mason stared at the phone. "What's tricky?"

"The body wasn't found on property that belonged to your mom. It was found on the lighthouse property. In the trees, just like you told us. This whole area is now a crime scene."

Rebecca understood. "Does that mean what I think it means?"

"Yes, ma'am. I apologize to the Preservation Society, but nothing can be done here until this case is completely closed. That could take months with all the property we'll have to search through, looking for additional evidence."

That bit of phrasing most likely came straight from Agent Hazzard. Or maybe it was from Dr. Montgomery. Either way, it was perfectly worded to calm Mason down as it addressed his immediate fears.

"That means that no one can tear the lighthouse down?" Gracie's voice shook with emotion and her hands clutched Bob's shirt.

Rebecca smiled. "That's right, ma'am."

Bob clapped his hands. "The lighthouse is safe?"

Rebecca nodded. "The lighthouse is protected."

Chuck picked up on what they were doing. "Thank you, God. Our beautiful Noble Lighthouse is safe."

Mason appeared stunned. "You believe me that my mother didn't leave me?"

Rebecca nodded. "We know your mother didn't leave you but was taken from you instead."

Mason closed his eyes and lowered the gun to his side. "Then I should go to the scientists so they can take my DNA and make sure it's a fifty percent match to my mom."

Rebecca didn't allow herself the sigh of relief she wanted.

"That's a wonderful idea." She licked her lips. "When we go out, you're going to need to wear handcuffs, like you made me wear."

He blinked at her. "Why?"

"It's so that everyone out there knows that you don't want to hurt anyone."

Mason thought that over for only a moment before he nodded. "That's fine. I scared people."

"Can you set the gun down so I can put the handcuffs on you?"

Rebecca didn't dare breathe until the gun was on a cardboard box. He put her phone beside it. She pulled the key from the pouch in her waistband as she walked over to him and unlocked her cuffs.

He frowned. "You could get away the whole time?"

She smiled. "Yes, but I knew you wouldn't hurt me."

A tear slid down his cheek. "I didn't want to hurt anyone."

Rebecca turned him around and secured his wrists behind his back. Picking up her phone, she said the words she'd been wanting to say for hours. "We're coming out."

In an amazing show of solidarity, Gracie rose to her feet and moved to Mason's side, hooking her arm through his. It was against protocol...*but fuck it*.

Rebecca placed a hand on Mason's shoulder. "Ready?"

He nodded. "Yeah."

As Rebecca ushered Mason outside, Gracie on his arm and Bob and Chuck behind them, she inhaled deeply for the first time in hours. While they all had been held against their will, Mason had been Shadow's hostage as well, held by his memories here.

Hoyt was the first to meet them. She handed her prisoner over. "Let's get a DNA sample and rush it through the system. I think Mason has waited long enough for answers."

"Yeah, Boss."

As Hoyt led Mason away, officers and paramedics rushed forward to tend to the hostages.

Hazzard shot her a little salute. "Good job."

Was it?

The whole situation had been so bizarre. Saving a lighthouse no one even knew was at risk of being sold and finding a runaway wife that had never left. Many questions had been answered, but several remained.

And Rebecca still had a killer to apprehend.

34

"The workday just never ends, does it?" Rebecca accepted the bottle of water she was passed and took a few chugs, watching as the SWAT team packed up, not at all grumpy that they hadn't been needed after sitting around for more than a day in the burning sun.

She turned her attention to the body disposal site. It'd been buried close to the lighthouse.

All the usual faces were there among the techs she'd come to know over the last several weeks. Bailey Flynn, medical examiner, and her assistant Margo Witt. Darian and a handful of state troopers who were glaring at the gawkers who'd moved their group closer as well.

"Well, what did you expect?" Benji rolled his eyes as he hung by her side. "You ended a hostage situation by opening a murder investigation, possibly three or more, and several cases of fraud."

"The paperwork on this is going to be so messy." Her complaints were cut off as Viviane ran up and gave her a hug, startling her. "What are you doing here?" It was hard to talk while having her neck hugged so hard.

"Not freaking out, in case you were wondering." Viviane finally released her and looked at Benji with a curiosity she didn't attempt to hide.

"Benji, this is Viviane, my friend and dispatcher extraordinaire. Viviane, this is Benji, my old partner."

"Old partner like…" Viviane bobbed her eyebrows.

Rebecca shook her head. "Like Special Agent partner. From the FBI."

"I'm just tagging along because I know the only way to spend any time with Rebecca is if it's on the job. She really doesn't know how to relax." Benji reached out to shake Viviane's hand. "I didn't think I'd be spending so much of it listening to her on a speaker talking down a gunman while she was handcuffed, though."

"I can agree with you on both counts." Viviane faked a glare at Rebecca.

"Hey, at least the day after tomorrow is Saturday. How about I take the whole day off and give you a tour of the island?" She grinned at Viviane and they both laughed. Weekends were their busiest days.

Benji frowned. "You're not going to get a whole day off, are you?"

He could still read her so well. "I can try…if we can wrap up this case before then."

He rubbed his hands together. "Okay, then. What do we need to do?"

Rebecca eyed her friendly dispatcher sheepishly. She batted her lashes for extra effect.

Viviane threw up her hands. "Oh, heck. I know that look. Whaddaya need, Boss?"

"I need you to head back to the office and do some additional research for me. Go through the property records to see who bought Paddy's Pub and J.J.'s home. I'm pretty sure you're going to see Coastal Properties was the buyer."

"You got it." Viviane disappeared as Rebecca returned her attention to the dig site.

Darian glanced up from where he was watching a tech sort through the ground covering. "Good to see you survived, sir."

"Good job finding this so quickly." Rebecca moved to stand opposite him from the crime scene but didn't bother to duck under the tape. There was nothing she could do here, really, except ask some questions and take pictures.

"The dogs did all the work. I hope Hoyt remembers to buy that box of treats for them."

"If not, I've got a box in my trunk." She watched Bailey remove dirt from the bones. The grave was deep, at least five feet. Considering the age of the trees surrounding the grave, the upturned dirt of Maria's final resting spot had likely been camouflaged by the new plantings. It was no wonder they hadn't seen anything back then.

"Are your food options down here in such a sad state that you have to resort to dog biscuits when on the job, Sheriff?"

Rebecca smiled at the voice and looked around until she spotted Rhonda Lettinger from the Norfolk branch of the Virginia State Police approaching. Darian offered her a nod as well.

"I keep them in my cruiser to feed stray dogs or ones that don't want me getting too close to their owners or homes. Or just when I see a cute pup." Rebecca stuck out her hand. "Lettinger, what brings you to our fair island today?"

"I heard you had some festivities out here and thought I'd stop by to see if you found any more of my missing bodies. Especially since you've been checking into two old cases in my jurisdiction."

"We're not sure what we have yet." Bailey spoke without looking up from the hole that was being excavated. "Despite what you may have been told, we don't know for certain yet if this is even a woman, let alone Maria Noble Alton."

"Was Hoyt telling the truth about the necklace? Or was that just to calm Mason down?"

"Oh, the necklace was found." Darian held up an evidence bag with a gold necklace inside. "That's why we believe this is the missing woman."

"Any way of knowing if the death was a homicide?" Rebecca crossed her fingers.

Bracing her arm on the other side, Bailey leaned into the grave once again. "The skull is fractured, but I'll have to do some tests to see if they were ante- or postmortem."

That was what Rebecca had figured. It'd been worth asking. On to the next question. "Darian, I didn't see Dennis Alton when I got out. Has he been around?"

"No, sir. Just me and the staties. And the dogs." He pointed to where the barks were growing distant.

"That reminds me." Benji shook his finger at her. "While you were off bearding the lion in his den and giving all of us heart attacks in addition to a slew of leads, I dug a bit more into the sale of the Altons' house. Turns out, Dennis Alton didn't just sell Mason's land to Coastal Properties. After the developer tried to get Maria to sell, Dennis went to work for them part-time. He earned a few hefty commissions for finding new properties for CP to purchase and develop."

That bastard.

Rebecca took a last sip of water. "If he's guilty, you know he's on top of the news for updates, so sooner than later would be the best time to pay him a visit." She crushed the bottle in her hand before keying her radio. "Hey, Greg, do you have your ears on, over?"

"Yeah, Sheriff, what do you need?"

"See if you can find where Dennis Alton is staying."

"Sure thing. I'll let you know what I find, over."

Rebecca needed to talk to Mason's dad. He had some questions to answer.

35

"You've got to be kidding me." Rebecca didn't bother hiding her annoyance as she watched the reporter making a beeline for her. With an irritated sigh, she ducked under the crime scene tape.

"What is it?" Darian looked around, then frowned as he saw the man approaching. "Who's that?"

"He's with the Richmond newspaper. I forget which one. He keeps wanting to talk to me."

Bailey popped her head up out of the hole. "Rebecca, come take a look."

Rebecca took the excuse and cautiously stepped closer, remembering her lesson on adipocere and deeply hoping she wasn't stepping in any. It wasn't called corpse wax for nothing. The water-insoluble material mainly consisted of saturated fatty acids that leached out of the corpse and could be incredibly slick in situations like this. Just her luck, she'd fall on her ass in front of the reporter.

"We've just reached the hip bones." Gingerly, Bailey lifted them out of the ground. "The pelvic inlet and sciatic notch appear female." Twisting it around, she showed it to Rebecca before handing it to her assistant to bag.

"Not sure you should be swinging your hips that much at work, Bailey." Darian put his palms to his cheeks, pretending to hide a blush. He then turned serious. "There's a gap in the barrier." He nodded to where the reporter was peeking into the excavation site. "Want me to close it up?"

Bailey nodded. "Please do. Don't want the civvies to see my thighs."

Considering Bailey's butt was sticking up in the air, Rebecca couldn't help but snicker. The techs were sorting and bagging. The staties were patrolling the borders of the crime scene. The cadaver dogs were finishing up the search. Darian was there to keep an eye on everything, and Hoyt was getting Mason Alton's paperwork sorted.

"I suppose I could find a few minutes for this guy." Rebecca hated the idea, hated talking about herself, and was already embarrassed someone would be writing a story about her. But better to get it over with. Certainly better than having him follow her around for the next couple of days until she snapped.

"Do you want me to get rid of him?" Benji offered. "I already talked to him once. He seems fairly harmless. None of his questions were off-color or anything."

"You already talked to him?" That annoyed Rebecca. The only thing worse than talking about herself to the press was someone else talking about her behind her back.

Benji frowned. "He asked me a few questions, just basic stuff like years spent training, your qualifications. Nothing he couldn't look up on his own. He just wanted someone he could quote. Apparently, he's doing a feature article on you. Might even be some kind of 'woman in power' thing."

"Ugh, I hope it's nothing creepy." She stepped away from Bailey and made her way over to where the reporter was waiting as if it were Christmas and she was Santa Claus.

"If he asks to take pictures, I can accidentally throw a shovelful of mud at him." Darian seemed entirely too happy about that idea.

"Just don't mess up the crime scene." Rebecca shot him a look over her shoulder, and he grinned and grabbed a spare shovel.

"Sheriff West, do you have a few minutes to talk? I just have a few questions." Oscar Toullaine leaned forward eagerly enough that the nearest state trooper reached a hand out to keep him from falling through the caution tape.

"Very few. Make it quick." Maybe he wouldn't want to move forward with the article if she was boring.

"Great. From all reports, you've already caught a ring of child smugglers, four murderers who killed nearly a dozen victims, and helped the island withstand a devastating hurricane. And now you've talked down a madman with no lives lost in a hostage situation that lasted more than a day and are digging into a decade-old cold case that you've just unearthed. How does it feel to be the shining new superstar of justice in such a small, remote tourist town?"

"Tired," Rebecca answered without thinking, and that proved just how exhausted she was. She tried to think back on how many victims there'd been since she took over, and her mind rebelled, not wanting to ponder that or do the math.

He laughed before she could think of a stronger response.

Who the hell are his sources? Do I have a leak in the department? One more thing to ponder.

"I'm sure you are. To what do you attribute your unparalleled success here?"

"Teamwork. I have a tremendous staff of deputies who make my job easier."

Toullaine frowned, and she felt a wee bit of joy at his dissatisfaction. It was petty, yet fun.

"But surely your FBI training has helped you deal with these problems."

"Sure. Training always helps. That was why when the hurricane approached, I relied on my deputies and an experienced, retired deputy to advise and help me make the decisions needed at the time. I could not have done my job without their support, knowledge, training, and experiences. Sheriff Wallace, my predecessor, assembled a stand-up group of professionals."

"But—"

She waved a hand at his recorder. "If you want a quote for what I attribute my success to, you can write this down. My team here at the Shadow Island Sheriff's Department is the reason we've been able to handle so many cases and get justice for the victims."

That line must not have been as good as she thought it was because he sighed. "Did you decide to take this job because of your connection with this island? Didn't you vacation here with your parents before they were killed?"

"Have you been following me since I was a child?" Not waiting for an answer to her snarky rhetorical question, Rebecca shifted the topic. "I took this job because it was offered to me."

"Do you find it harder to do your job after exposing Senator Bill Morley and his possible connection with your parents' deaths?"

Her heart picked up speed, and she strove to keep her irritation from her face. "This is my first time being a sheriff, so I have no comparison to make."

Toullaine turned off the recorder and sighed. "Could you at least comment on the controversy you stirred up with the senator? That would give a lot more flavor to my story and shine a better light on the hard work you're doing here with so much political baggage in your past."

Rebecca reached out, turned on the recorder, and held it up to her mouth, making Toullaine smile again. She made sure she enunciated clearly while looking him dead in his eyes.

"No." She turned the device off and passed it back to him. The state trooper's shoulders bounced as he silently laughed. "Now I really do need to get back to my job."

"Wait!"

"Have a good day, Mr. Toullaine." Rebecca walked off, and he did his best to keep up with her on his side of the tape line.

"Just a few more questions. What made you decide to move to this island? How did you convince the Select Board to promote you to sheriff over the other deputies who've been here longer?" He continued calling out questions until Darian put himself between the two of them.

"Look, man, what makes us good at our job is that we don't get sidetracked. I respect that you have a job to do, but so do we. And your job is directly interfering with our ability to do ours. Feel free to interview all the bystanders. Heck, when we aren't so busy, we'll do our best to answer the questions we can. But we don't come down to where you're working and pester you while you're trying to write, do we?"

"What? No, of course not."

Rebecca almost laughed as Toullaine's eyebrows danced like drunk caterpillars.

Drunk caterpillars? Holy crap, I am tired. Taking a catnap in the front seat of the cruiser isn't enough to get through the next day anymore.

"Then how about you give us the same considerations? Sheriff West is quite literally ankle-deep in work, and you keep bombarding her with questions. She's the sheriff. Use your brain. You can call the station and make an appointment to talk with her. Show some professional courtesy."

Oscar opened his mouth a few times but couldn't come up with a response. Seeing that everyone was watching him with stony, unfriendly faces, he finally gave up and walked back the way he'd come.

"I appreciate the interference," Rebecca smiled at Darian, "but I can handle guys like him."

"We all know you *can*," Darian stressed the last word with a devious smile. "But we *get* to. We never get to be rude to reporters at any other time or tell them to go fuck off. So just give us this one chance. Please, Boss?"

Rebecca chuckled. "Plausible deniability."

"Yes, sir."

36

Turning on my signal, I pulled onto the gravel parking lot. No one was around, so this was an excellent place to wait and watch. There was a lot for me to think about. The chirp of crickets and croak of frogs resumed as my car engine cooled.

The stench of dirt and fetid water. I hated it so much. It was just one of the many reasons I despised this place. Still, my work brought me here, and I was more than happy to help turn this bog into a suitable place to live.

Things could've gone better. I'd hoped to have everything wrapped up yesterday. But I had to admit, they didn't go badly either. It'd been a real surprise to see how quickly and smoothly the locals here responded to each new problem. I'd been told the sheriff usually turned a blind eye to most things. Because he didn't care or just didn't want to deal with the paperwork, I didn't know. And didn't care.

Of course, these small-town hicks hadn't found my latest surprise, not yet. I knew how to cover my tracks, but again, it was better if I didn't leave any evidence at all. No matter how hard they dug.

From where I was sitting, I watched them still milling about in the trees. It seemed like they'd been out there all day, swapping out people and bringing in fresh ones. The roads teeming with official vehicles driving both ways. They seemed to be wrapping up now, at least.

Another state trooper drove up the road, and I watched him head back to civilization. The state cops had broken down the command post near the parking lot and were now tramping through the woods and sorting through the dirt.

The baying of the dogs was another nuisance. Not just the noise they were making, but the fact that they hadn't left yet. Dogs weren't something I'd planned on. Of course, if my plans had been followed at the beginning, there wouldn't have been anything for them to find.

It didn't matter anymore. I'd already packed my bags, and I was ready to get out of here. The city was waiting for me, as were the necessities one could find there. Clubs, bars, hotels with jacuzzies, room service, and concierges who didn't ask intrusive questions.

I watched another cop car drive past and checked my rearview mirror. The sun still had a few more hours before it would go down. Then the crews working in the woods would have to pack it up and leave too.

Once they were gone and things settled down again, I could put the finishing touches on my work and move on. Mason was no longer a worry, and neither was this town. It was hard to believe I'd managed to do this well with that ass dragging me down.

There was no one left to tie me to anything from the past. Soon, I could leave this tiny town and never look back. Onward to better things, I always said. I only had to kill a few more hours until the situation was perfect, which worked for me, since I was hungry anyway. For a moment, I debated leaving town. There was a better selection of restaurants off this island, but then I'd have to return. Wasn't worth it.

I started my car and drove back the way I'd come just minutes ago.

Driving into town didn't turn my stomach as it usually did. Knowing this would probably be the last time I'd have to helped a lot. I'd already taken everything I wanted from this place and could keep moving to greener pastures. Or at least, less run-down and worn-out ones.

Tourists flooded the roads, making traffic crawl as they all sought out dinner plans. If only there were someplace good to eat. But as I knew, there wasn't. All that was available were greasy mom-and-pop type places.

Maybe I could at least find a fast-food chain and get a burger and fries I could eat in my car as I waited for twilight. Traffic crawled forward as I hoped for a familiar sign with those golden arches. As I pulled up beside a parking lot, I saw a truck I recognized. When the driver got out, the logo on his back confirmed I was right.

This was a perfect opportunity. I pulled onto the shoulder and turned into the parking lot, honking my horn a few times to get the man's attention. He and the other men he'd met up with all turned to stare as I parked next to them.

"Hey, guys!"

The first man smiled and waved, even though the others still looked confused. That was fine. They didn't know me, and that didn't matter. It wasn't like they were the type of people I would hang out with if given a choice. They were all working men, with dirt ground into their hands and under their nails.

But that didn't matter. I knew their type and how to talk to them. Soon enough, they'd like me just fine. I got out of my car and walked over to meet them.

"Hey, man. Hard day?" I swung my hand around for a

hard slap to his palm. Then we shook as I nodded my chin up at the men gathered behind him.

"Well, the delays aren't helping things. That's for sure." He rolled his eyes. "I bet we didn't even really need to leave."

"Yeah, but we all know bad days happen. Things out of our control are always waiting to screw us up. If it's not the rain, it's the sun. Am I right? Tell you what, let me buy you guys the first round." That lightened the mood immediately, and the men gave grudging smiles and nods. "Let's go see what this small town has to offer us."

And just like that, I was accepted into the group. Their headman liked me, and I was buying them drinks. That was good enough for their simple minds.

I led them inside as they laughed and chatted about what a strange day it'd been. It only took a few questions before they turned to talk about the weirdest things they'd seen on the job before, and no one was in a bad mood. Each one of them tried to one-up the other. And everything that had bothered them about today was soon forgotten.

Tonight would be a good night for them. That I could make sure of. And once I got these guys nicely tucked into the bar, I could go back to the construction site to drop off the last man on this project. They'd be so hungover tomorrow, they wouldn't even notice a few things being out of place.

37

"Boss, we're here."

Rebecca opened her eyes and stretched so hard she whacked her wrist on the passenger side window. She felt like a can of hammered Spam. Her eyes burned, her muscles ached, and her feet were throbbing now that she'd been off them for a few minutes.

"I wish I could nap like Darian does. He always looks so revived after he wakes up." Using both hands, she smoothed her hair back and redid her ponytail. Just because she felt like a wreck didn't mean she had to look like one. About the only relief she felt so far was when she'd learned that Eleanor Weever was doing very well and was expected to make a full recovery.

The neon sign of the Tidepool Motel wasn't lit up yet, as the sun was just starting to lower in the sky. Hopefully, this would be the last thing they had to do tonight. Tracking down Dennis Alton to try and get a confession out of him wasn't a great idea when she was this tired, so she'd come up with an alternative plan.

They would detain Dennis Alton overnight, offering him

a plush cell on the mainland. Once he was settled, she'd go home and get a good night's sleep while Bailey did her thing. This plan of action would keep Alton from fleeing, give her time to recuperate, and let him sit and stew while he wondered what evidence they had against him.

Unless he was feeling guilty enough to just confess right off the bat. That would be nice. Whichever course of action took her home to her bed the soonest was okay with her.

Hoyt, already out of the driver's seat, knocked on her window. "You coming?"

With a hearty sigh, Rebecca rolled out of the cruiser, cursing when her feet hit concrete. She needed a better pair of shoes.

Slamming the door behind her, she stalked toward the manager's office. "Let's hope he tries to resist."

Hoyt rubbed his hands together. "Any man who can kill his wife and abandon his child deserves all the 'stop resisting' we can dish out."

She yanked open the lobby door. "I'm betting on him being the one who told Mason the lighthouse was being torn down too."

"Ya think?"

"He works with Coastal Properties, right?"

"And he's someone Mason's known, someone he would trust, like the doctor talked about, right?"

"Yeah. But he didn't actually point any fingers at his father. He couldn't fathom going there." She lowered her voice as they got closer to the manager and pulled out her badge. "Is Dennis Alton still here?" She slapped down the warrant.

The young man standing at the counter was nearly shaking as he pulled up the information. Rebecca bet it was because she looked as furious and crabby as she felt.

"Room 206, second floor, front side, ma'am." He held out a key with a room tag on it and pointed with his other hand.

"Thanks." Rebecca took the key and spun around, catching Hoyt off guard.

He stumbled back a bit and pushed open the door. "That was quick."

She shrugged. "I think I scared him."

Hoyt's gaze traveled over her flyaway hair and the ponytail she could already feel slipping, then settled on the scowl marring her forehead.

"Your reputation's getting around. You've been in more gunfights than anyone else here. While on the force."

That *on the force* covered Darian and his time in the military, but she couldn't help but wonder if he was thinking of anyone else as well. Now wasn't the time to dwell on it, though. She just wanted to get this task completed so she could clock out and be done with work for at least eight hours.

The sun was setting at their backs as she went up the stairs, casting their shadows down through the treads. The sidewalk below bustled with folks in no hurry to be anywhere, and Rebecca found herself envious. An evening breeze carried the calls of gulls riding the currents.

Once this errand was completed, Rebecca could go home, take a fast shower, and fall into bed. Maybe after a good night's sleep, these interlocking cases would somehow make sense.

Right now, things made as much sense as Mason's unhinged rantings.

"Why do you think Wallace didn't look into the possibility that Maria was dead? Or follow up with her mother?" The questions had been spinning in her head for hours.

Hoyt paled. "I don't know." He shook his head and wouldn't meet her gaze. "We keep learning new things about him, things I never thought I'd learn. Half the time, it points to him being the hero I thought he was. The other half makes me wonder if he hid things, to protect us like he said, but also because he was corrupt to the core. I know which way I want it to lean, but that won't make things right."

A thread of paranoid worry slithered through Rebecca, and she studied his face. When it came down to it, would Hoyt have her back, even if it meant exposing Wallace as a dirty cop? She didn't have any skin in the game, but he'd been friends with the man most of his life. How far would he or the other deputies go to protect the memory of their friend?

She honestly didn't know. And if Hoyt was being truthful with himself, he probably didn't either. His reluctance to look at her was telling.

"There was a lot of money to be made with that land sale. That kind of money can turn a lot of blind eyes."

Dammit. She was so tired she was speaking without thinking.

"I'm sure it can. But if Wallace ever had money, I never saw any sign of it. At least, he didn't spend it on anything flashy. Maybe I didn't know him as well as I thought, but one thing I do know." He met her gaze, his lips playing with a smile. "If Alden Wallace had gotten any kind of big money, he'd have paid someone else to paint his house last year."

Surprised by the comment, Rebecca chuckled.

Hoyt joined her, but not as boisterously. His laugh held a hint of pain that sobered her up quickly.

"I can't fault that logic." They reached the second-floor landing. "That's his room over there."

Before she took another step, she glanced left and right, making sure no one was watching them or likely to get in the way if things turned bad. The landing was poured concrete on metal bracers and frames, swallowing up all sound and vibrations of anyone walking along it. A line of bland beige walls broken up by white curtains and brown doors stretched either way. There were no signs of anyone.

All the sensible people are out getting dinner or relaxing on the beach. If only I were one of them. I really need a vacation from my vacation.

They walked up to the door together, then split so they could stand on either side. Rebecca was at the doorknob, Hoyt the hinge. She listened closely while he tried to peek through the shut curtains. After a few seconds, he shook his head. His hand settled on his gun.

So did hers.

Her heart picked up speed and all her senses went on high alert. Something, some instinct, was picking up danger. She looked around but couldn't see anything obvious that would've set her senses on full alert. Regardless, she heeded them.

Using the side of her fist, Rebecca pounded on the door hard enough to shake the *Do Not Disturb* tag hanging from the handle. "Sheriff's department, open up!"

Nothing.

She waited fifteen seconds before knocking again. "Sheriff's department. Dennis Alton, open the door or we're coming in."

Still no response.

Pulling her gun, she glanced at Hoyt. "Ready?"

He pulled his weapon and nodded. The lock was sticky, but she managed to turn the knob without any resistance. Raising her leg, she kicked the door open hard enough that it crashed into the wall.

Hoyt rushed forward, and she was right behind him, covering the corners of the room.

There wasn't a lot of room to clear. Other than the single bed that Hoyt was already stepping around, there were only two possible blind spots at the half wall and the bathroom in the back. Rebecca rushed to the bathroom, gritting her teeth as she threw open the shower curtain.

The movie *Psycho* had scarred her for life.

"Clear."

Back in the bedroom, Rebecca watched Hoyt kick the bed before going down to check underneath.

He shook his head. "Clear."

Well, shit.

The room was messy but empty. There were no clothes or suitcases. No shoes were left by the door. And all the drawers were left hanging open. It looked like Dennis Alton had made his escape.

She shoved her sidearm into her holster and reached for her gloves. "But not clean."

Hoyt stepped up beside her. "Well. Dammit on a waffle."

She chuckled at the curse. It was a new one.

At the foot of the bed, Rebecca noticed an anomaly that interrupted the carpet's ugly pattern. Pulling on gloves, she crouched down and placed a finger on the side of the small puddle. The surface was dry, but when she pushed harder, a tacky red substance appeared.

"That blood?"

Rebecca nodded. That was an easy question to answer. The harder one was…

Is this Dennis Alton's blood or someone else's?

38

After retrieving the camera from the SUV, Rebecca made her way back into the room as Hoyt put up the tape and called in the crime scene techs. One step at a time, she took pictures from all angles. She had no idea what they were really dealing with here. Just in case, she put out an APB for Dennis Alton. His car was still in the parking lot, and she called for a tow truck to get it hauled away for closer inspection.

While going through the room taking pictures, she'd found a clumsily scrawled note on the dresser next to the television. The paper bore the motel's logo, as did the pen beside it.

I killed Maria and talked Mason into doing what he did. I wanted him arrested so he'd be forced to go back into the hospital. I never meant for him to hurt anyone, and now I'm going to swim until I can't swim anymore. Dennis Alton.

Rebecca didn't believe a word of it.

As much as she'd hoped for a confession when she got here, this didn't sit right. The handwriting was so sloppy, it could've been written by anyone, including a dyslexic doctor with a hand cramp. It looked like someone had written with the pen in their fist, or with their nondominant hand.

So why was it left in the first place? And by who?

To cover all bases, she made a note to find a sample of Alton's handwriting from someone like a landlord or employer. They could at least compare the signatures.

And why were all his belongings missing? Had he taken a swim with his suitcase?

Who packs to commit suicide?

Once he was done securing the crime scene, Hoyt said he was going downstairs to check with the manager on duty for any video they might have.

"See if you can get a copy of his signature from his check-in papers too. And see if anyone else was staying with him. That would help speed things up a bit. And something tells me this needs a rush job."

"On it, Boss." Hoyt walked out, and she heard him greet someone outside.

With her pictures taken, she stepped out to see who he was talking to.

Justin Drake, one of the techs she'd enjoyed working with, waved as he stepped onto the second-floor landing. He was in a fresh set of coveralls, not the full bunny suit she'd seen him wearing earlier.

"Hey, Sheriff West. Good job catching us before we made it off the island. We get paid per call out at this hour of the day, no matter if we're an hour or five minutes away."

Rebecca smiled and moved out of his way. "Good to know I had my timing down pat."

He studied her face. "You guys have been on your feet since early this morning, right? Hoyt looks a bit worse for wear than you do, but you still look more than a bit wilted. No offense meant."

Rebecca checked the mirror and winced. *Wilted* was

putting it nicely. "We've been working since yesterday morning, actually. Caught a couple catnaps in the cruiser, but let's just say I'm looking forward to getting home."

"I bet."

She strode over to the dresser. "Found this note. I've photographed it so I can get the signature analyzed."

He took out an evidence bag and read the note. "That's… weird." He turned a full circle, taking in the room. "Where's his stuff?"

"Exactly. We've already checked, and none of his belongings are in his vehicle either."

Justin grimaced. "I guess it's possible he took everything with him into the water. Maybe thought it'd help him sink faster."

Rebecca had thought of that too. She shrugged. "Guess it's my job to find out."

Justin grinned. "Better you than me."

Stomping feet moved toward the room. Hoyt appeared in the doorway. "Got the handwriting. It's not a match. Not even close. And the cameras are fake. They only have the ones in the lobby and by the dumpster. Here." He handed over a cup of coffee. There was no lid, and it looked like burned hell. "They had a pot in the lobby, but I think it was brewed this morning."

Ignoring the taste, Rebecca took a long drink. "Thanks. We could be here another few hours."

"Aww, is this intruding on plans you had for a wild night?" Hoyt took a sip and frowned like it'd bitten him.

"Yup, a wild and crazy night of cuddling with my pillows and comforter. Maybe even a meal while sitting down at a table. An affair with my shower, for sure."

Hoyt yawned, and to her supreme gratitude, it triggered her to yawn too.

"You think he really offed himself?"

"Not a chance." Rebecca tried to imagine a man walking out into the water carrying a suitcase without a hundred tourists watching. "I'll alert the Coast Guard, of course, but I just don't see it."

"You think he killed his wife?"

"Yeah. According to Mason's story, he probably did. But even with all the new information we've gotten from our young man with a thing for sleuthing, it still feels like we're missing something."

"Like what?"

"Like, why did Alton show up at the lighthouse today? Is Richmond Vale involved somehow or just looking to sell out the island for a quick buck? My background check on Jeff Benton this morning came back squeaky clean. Almost too clean, if you know what I mean. And who told Mason about the demolition? And we're waiting to hear from Viviane if both Pearce and Gossard are connected to Coastal Properties. I think we have most of the pieces, but they're not assembled properly. It's like one of those puzzles that has more than one solution."

She took another drink of her coffee and ignored Hoyt's grimace. This was going to wreak hell in her stomach, but it wasn't the worst she'd had. And at the end of the day, coffee was coffee.

"Well, we got a new crime scene. The sad thing about crime scenes is they always give us more information."

"Hopefully, this one will supply us with the pieces we're missing. If it doesn't, we're all out of leads, and I'm all out of ideas."

39

"Need a sounding board?"

Rebecca knew that voice. She pushed away from the cruiser she'd been leaning against, shaking herself from thoughts so deep she hadn't even heard Benji approach.

She grinned. "Are you following me around? And please tell me one of those is mine." She nodded to the cardboard drink carrier in his hand before scowling at the cup with the tag for an herbal tea bag hanging out of it. "And don't you dare give me that one."

"I wouldn't dare." He handed a different cup over to her. "Of course I'm following. I came to visit you. Remember?" He handed a second cup to Hoyt. "I'm not sure how you take your coffee, man, sorry. But I brought creamers and sugar, just in case."

"Thanks. Black is fine."

Benji nodded toward the motel. "Want to talk about it?"

"There's not much to say. An empty room and missing suspect. Forged letter from Dennis Alton that says he's responsible for Maria's death and Mason taking hostages, and that he's going to commit suicide. Plus, blood on the carpet that doesn't fit a suicide at all. Oh, and he packed."

"Well, the troopers found a giant pile of clothes and personal items in the dumpster over by the convenience store next door to where I got the coffee. They told me about it as I walked up. I guess they thought I was working the case with you, but I directed them to tell the techs. That could be your man's missing clothes, at least. Which doesn't bode well for his survival."

"Or it's his way of distracting us from his disappearance."

Benji tapped his cup against hers. "True. It appears he packed for a long trip, according to the troopers."

That didn't feel right either.

"Who would benefit from Dennis and Maria's deaths and the incarceration of Mason?" Hoyt asked. "It seems to me someone has it out for that entire family."

"Maybe it's an old blood feud, and the other family was just waiting until the Altons came back before they attacked the rest of the family."

Rebecca whirled to find Oscar Toullaine creeping up behind them like the snake he was. She sighed and eyed the man warily. He was like a leech she just couldn't shake. "That sounds like something that would sell plenty of newspapers but rarely has anything to do with reality. What are you doing up here, Mr. Toullaine?"

He shrugged. "Just following my nose."

"No comment."

He frowned at her. "I didn't ask a question."

"Preemptive strategy."

To her surprise, he waved that aside. "I've already written the article, so there's no need for more questions. I just wanted to pop over to let you know that. Also, my editor seems happy with it too. I'll let you know when it gets published."

He watched one of the crime scene techs carry something to the van. "It's hard to believe there's another murder scene so soon after the last one."

"Crime scene," she corrected. "Nothing to write home about."

Oscar laughed at the wordplay.

Her phone buzzed. It was a message from Ryker, and she pressed her lips together to hide a smile.

Dinner?

Her stomach growled, and she noticed the time. It was nearly eleven. *Yes. Free in about an hour. That too late?*

A smiling emoji was followed by, *Sounds good. Call when you're ready.*

"Have a good night, all three of you." The reporter stuck out his hand.

Rebecca gave it a quick shake. "Drive safe, Mr. Toullaine."

When Hoyt yawned, she patted his shoulder. "Why don't you head home and get some sleep?"

"You sure, Boss? I got more sleep than you did."

After joining him in the damn yawn despite her best efforts to keep it down, Rebecca said, "I'm sure." She held up her cup. "I've got a few more minutes left in me. Locke's had most of the day to sleep and will be on in a couple of hours. He and Darian can handle things tonight."

"You gonna go home?" Hoyt glanced over at Benji as he yawned behind his cup.

"Unlike some tea drinkers here," she frowned at her old partner, "I can pull my own weight."

"You're a workaholic, you mean. And herbal tea is good for you, unlike your sludge. I'll have you know this is a white tea with peaches and bergamot." He lifted his pinky finger before taking a dainty sip.

Rebecca laughed as they slipped into their old routine of

bickering. "I'm going to head to the office and tie up some loose ends."

Hoyt nodded. "I'll get to the office at seven. You sleep as late as you can."

Rebecca offered a fist, and her deputy bumped it. After thanking Benji for the coffee, Hoyt strode away.

She elbowed Benji. "Want to join me at the office? The techs will close up the scene." She noticed Justin at the van and walked over. "You guys got anything for us before we leave?"

"Nada." Justin ripped off his gloves and swiped the sweat from his forehead. "We're taking fingerprints. Got a stack of those in the usual places. Dressers, doorknobs, handles, and such. You want to take those with you and run them? I can already tell you we've got at least three different ones."

"Give me one of each. I'll start running them when I get back to the office." She ducked under the tape and took the ones he handed her.

"You're leaving now?"

"Yeah, the troopers will stay, but I can send Locke over, too, if you think you'll need him."

Justin wrinkled his nose. "The troopers are fine."

Interesting.

"You don't like Locke?"

Justin shrugged. "I just don't think he takes his job very seriously."

Rebecca's anger at Locke's incompetence hit a new level. She'd seen how he acted at the lighthouse, but this was something completely different. When incompetence happened often enough that the crime scene techs knew about it and were bothered, Rebecca needed to address it.

"I'll send Darian over, if you'd rather."

Justin pulled on a fresh pair of gloves. "We'd appreciate that, Sheriff."

Rebecca gave a sharp nod and said her farewells. She had some staffing issues to deal with back at the station.

40

The station was too quiet. Rebecca cupped a hand around her mouth and yelled, "Darian!"

"Yes, sir!"

Benji shot her a confused stare as he followed her through the half door into the back offices at the station. Neither Melody nor Viviane was at the counter, and she couldn't honestly remember who was covering this shift.

"Can you go babysit the techs at the Tidepool Motel for an hour or so?"

"Yes, ma'am."

Benji's eyebrows quirked together, and he started to laugh but swallowed it down as Darian approached them. "Heya, Agent Huang, you still hanging around?"

"Hard to catch up with her when she's always running off to the next scene."

Darian laughed. "You might have to handcuff her again."

"That might be the only way to get her to stay in one place long enough to have a chat."

"By the way, Mason's shrink is in back with him. He was

having a bad spell, so I let her into the interrogation room so she could comfort him."

Rebecca's jaw sagged. "He's still here?"

Darian's eyes widened. "You didn't know? Sorry. He asked if he could wait here until he could speak to you."

Let me guess. Locke was supposed to let me know.

She blew out a breath. "I need to do a few things, then I'll go talk to him."

Benji turned to watch Darian exit the building as Rebecca refilled her cup. "Did I hear him right? He called you *sir* and *ma'am* back-to-back?"

Rebecca shrugged. "Yeah, that's Darian. He's Army through and through. Anytime I tell him to do anything, he calls me sir. When I call his name, he answers with a 'yes, sir.' When he addresses me, he calls me ma'am. I think his military lingo just got stuck in his head. I'm not even sure if he knows he's doing it."

"Quite a crew you've got down here. But this is the office?" He didn't even have to turn his body to look over the bullpen and kitchenette that was made up of one table next to a floating sink mounted on the wall with all the pipes showing.

"This is the main office. Mine is over here. I've even got a snazzy new chair. I may have broken the old chair during a, er…*discussion* I was having. Had to get a new one. Worked out, though. The new one has lumbar support."

"Oh, that discussion sounds like something I want to know more about." Rebecca's glare told him he wouldn't get the details from her, so he changed the topic. "Where's the rest of your staff?"

Rebecca shrugged and motioned for him to follow her back. "You've met almost everyone. Greg, Darian, Hoyt, and Viviane. Well, you haven't met Locke or Melody yet. She's on floating hours with Viviane this week." Saying that, she finally remembered that Melody must have simply transferred dispatch to their third-party service so she could take her meal break.

She walked into her office and waved her arm around. "Welcome to my domain."

"You need sleep. You're starting to get silly."

"*Pffft.*" Rebecca plopped down in her chair and sighed as she relaxed back into it. "I've been silly for a bit. Now I'm getting irritable."

Benji made a show of patting all his pockets before he sat down across from her. "I don't have any candy bars on me anymore. It's been too long since we were partners."

Rebecca laughed and shook her head, waking her computer up to sign in. "Hey, it's not like I have to rely on people to bring me meals to make sure I eat." Once logged in, she started scanning the fingerprint cards she'd brought.

It only took her a few moments to do so and get them started with a match search on the national registry for offenders.

"Boss, you in your office, over?" Darian's voice came over the radio.

Frowning, she picked it up. "Yes. Is something wrong?"

"Nope, just got a special delivery for you. I'll let him in."

This was strange enough that Rebecca got back on her feet and walked into the hallway to see who was being let inside.

Ryker smiled at her as he stepped into view. "Hey, there."

"Hey!" She glanced at the clock. It was nearly midnight. She felt terrible. "I'm so sorry, but I just got here."

He held up a brown paper bag. "I figured, but I wanted to make sure you ate."

Rebecca wanted to kiss him, and she didn't even know what food he'd brought. A snort from behind her stopped her before she could even take a step toward him.

"Shit." Ryker dropped his voice. "Are you in a meeting?"

Benji laughed. "Nope, not with anyone important. Just her old partner and friend."

Rebecca made the introduction. "Ryker, this is my old partner, Benji Huang. Benji, this is Ryker Sawyer, my friend and hero."

Ryker grinned down at her. "Hero, huh?"

"Well, you do keep helping me out." She motioned at the bag he was holding.

"Someone's got to make sure the sheriff's well taken care of. It's not just me, though. The whole town feels that way. I'm just the lucky guy who has an in."

"Good to know someone has her back." Benji stepped forward and held out his hand. "You don't want this one armed and hangry."

Ryker shook his hand with a smile. "I've heard about what she's done. I don't want her hangry at all. Even unarmed, she's still armed."

That might've been one of the best compliments she'd ever been given.

"Oh, we need to share stories sometime." Benji laughed and looked at Rebecca. With that look, she knew he had a stack of questions.

"Well, not to be rude or anything, but it's late. I just wanted to make sure you had a chance to eat before breakfast rolled around. Restaurants are going to be closing soon, and your pantry is pretty bare. Benji, it was good meeting you. Rebecca, I'll see you later."

She watched him walk away, enjoying every step.

"He knows how much food you have in your pantry?" Benji whispered in her ear. "You really have been working it since you got here."

She spun on Benji. "Not like that." She took her food and returned to her desk, eager to see what he'd brought her. As guilty as she felt for leaving Mason in the interrogation room, she knew she'd handle a conversation with him better with a full stomach. Once that was done, Agent Hazzard had agreed one of Rebecca's deputies could run Mason to the secure wing of the Coastal Ridge hospital for his psych eval and processing. "My landlord contracts with him for repairs and maintenance. He had to check the place out after the hurricane. Did you know the winds can get so strong they break the seals around windows?"

"Hey, if that's the line he has to use to come over, maybe you should give the guy a break and just ask him out already."

Rebecca pulled out the top container and frowned at the salad. The next one looked to be sliced watermelon. Below that was a piece of cardboard. "I did. He works nearly as many hours as I do. Especially since the storm. He does house repairs and runs his own business."

Benji leaned forward and peered at the containers of fruits and veggies. "Hmm, well, he clearly hasn't known you long enough yet."

Lifting the cardboard, she grinned as savory steam hit her nose. "Or maybe he has." She pulled out a hot container of steak cooked medium rare and sliced thin over a bed of cheddar mashed potatoes.

"What's that?"

He pointed at the cardboard in her hand. Flipping it over, she read the note scrawled in black marker. *Thank you for saving my brother, Bob. This is the meal he said he wanted after that long hot day in the lighthouse, so I thought it would suit your palette too. P.S. Don't let Ryker pretend he paid.*

"Who's Bob? One of the hostages?"

Rebecca nodded as she took out the container with the entrée and spotted the giant brownie covered in chocolate topping and strawberries. "Yeah, he'd nearly been shot. His shirt was the only casualty. Really lucky. And he helped carry Nora outside so she could be transported to the hospital by the paramedics. He told me later he thought it would be his last view of the sun before he died."

"Nice. We never get takeout delivered by grateful family members."

She surveyed all the food in front of her and then the plain paper bag. "Ya know, I'm not sure this is takeout. This might be a home-cooked meal. Do you know of any restaurants that serve watermelon slices like this?"

Benji shook his head. "Even better. Unless the family is mad at you for saving Bob. Then it could be risky. Maybe I should take that off your hands, just in case."

He started to reach for the food, but she snatched it away.

"Don't even think about it." She opened the tray of steak and popped a strip in her mouth. "I'll take my chances."

41

The late dinner was finished. Rebecca had even shared the watermelon with Benji. Darian had called in to say the techs were done, and he was going to make a loop at the beach before heading back, so she knew the footsteps from the back of the building couldn't be his. Besides, the steps were too soft for hard-soled military boots.

Dr. Montgomery appeared in the hallway. "I thought I heard voices out here. Good to know I don't need to take up residency with my patients."

Guilt tried to take a shot at Rebecca, but she refused to let it hit. She really had needed to eat.

"Is Mason settled down now?" Rebecca glanced at the clock and saw it was half past midnight.

"Settled may not be the best word for it. He's calmer, but he wants to talk to you. So I'm glad you came in so early."

Rebecca sighed. "Not early. Still on the clock. Have a seat. You've been back there for a while already."

The psychiatrist sat down and stretched her back. "Sounds like you work just as hard as we do. Some weeks, I don't even see my own bed. But that's not what matters right now. Mason has some things he wants to tell you. Things he hadn't even told me before because he thought they were too bad and that no one would believe him. I understand his problems better now. He's going to have to be recommitted. I hope so, anyway, and that prison isn't in his future."

Benji leaned forward, catching Rebecca's eye. "Are you saying he's not culpable for his actions?"

Dr. Montgomery held up both hands. "That's for a judge to decide. And not for me to talk about here and now."

That was a yes, but Rebecca knew the woman couldn't admit it. Since she hadn't said anything like this while trying to talk Mason out of the lighthouse, Rebecca couldn't help but wonder what had changed. It also meant he hadn't confessed to committing any crime. Otherwise, she would be free to talk about it.

"Benji, you wanna be my backup for an interrogation?"

He shrugged and stood up, straightening his shirt. "Sure, why not? I've got nowhere to be in the morning."

"Would you mind if I came with you?"

Rebecca eyed the doctor. "Don't you think that would be unethical?" It would undoubtedly make things confusing in court later.

"Not for the interrogation. Just when you walk back to get him. I can be a buffer until you begin questioning him."

Benji shot a look at her and gave a tiny nod. He would keep an eye on the doctor in case she tried anything. It wasn't likely, but that was what everyone thought before things went to shit.

"Let's go see what he has to say."

Rebecca led them out, stopping to grab a cup of water for the young man. Since the interrogation room doubled as the department's holding cell, detainees were permitted to roam freely when locked in the room alone. But they were careful not to leave anything behind that might be crafted into a weapon.

Mason smiled weakly at Dr. Montgomery from his seat at the table where one hand was handcuffed to a solid metal ring. Rebecca had hated to do that, but as volatile as the young man could be, it'd been necessary. Certainly, Dr. Montgomery never could have been left alone with him if he hadn't been restrained. Mason seemed to understand this, and that lessened Rebecca's guilt.

Benji closed the door, shutting Montgomery outside, before setting up the video system.

"You're going to record this?" Mason stared at the video camera.

"Yes. You wanted to get your story out, right?" Rebecca gestured to the device. "This is how we make sure everyone can hear what you have to say."

Mason nodded. "Yeah."

Though Rebecca knew Hoyt had read Mason his Miranda Rights, she did it again, wanting to get it recorded. "Do you understand the rights I just told you, Mason?"

"Yes." He nodded and looked directly into the camera. "To start, I want to apologize to everyone I hurt. I never wanted to hurt anyone. I just wanted the hurt to stop for me. I had to make sure no one tore the lighthouse down like they tore down my home. But I shouldn't have scared or hurt anyone to do that. I'm really sorry. Really sorry."

Rebecca shifted her gaze to Benji and raised an eyebrow at him. This was not the first time she'd started an interrogation with the suspect apologizing, but Mason's apology was the sincerest.

"That's very good of you to say, Mason."

"Ma always said you should first apologize, then explain what you did wrong, and only then can you say why you did what you did. Otherwise, it sounds like you're trying to make excuses. I'm not. I promise. I know not to hurt people. I know guns hurt people. But I got so angry, I couldn't think right, and that was wrong too. I shouldn't have gotten so angry."

"Is that what you wanted to tell me?"

Mason shook his head. "To you, I wanted to explain. I lost my mom. I lost Gramma. And my dad. Ma said I'd always have the land and the trees. But I didn't love the trees anymore. Not like Ma did. Not after they took her from me. After that, all I had left was the lighthouse. I couldn't let anyone take that from me too. I thought I had to do whatever it took to keep it."

"What made you think the lighthouse was in danger in the first place?" Rebecca watched him carefully.

Mason looked at Rebecca, then the camera. "Okay, well, Dad told me. I went to his apartment on the mainland. He told me about it. He said he had to sell our house, and it was too late for that, but not too late for the lighthouse."

Rebecca's heart squeezed at the young man's tears. "What else did your father say?"

"He said it was my fault. Because I was so bad. And the doctors and my meds cost so much." Mason's chin dipped to his chest. "My dad has sacrificed a lot to help me over the years, even though we don't really 'see eye to eye,' in his words."

Well, that cleared up her earlier suspicions. Mason was clueless about his father's real motivations.

"He told me the lighthouse was all we had left. Dad said the group home I'd been staying in wasn't going to take me back since I chose to leave. I'd be homeless. Without an anchor. All my links to my family, my history…they were all gone."

Tears dripped down Mason's face, and Rebecca handed

him a tissue. When he tried to dry his cheeks, the handcuffs got in the way.

Screw it.

Pulling the small key from her pocket, she reached over and unlocked the cuffs. To her surprise, Benji didn't seem to disagree with her actions.

"I was so scared." Mason blew his nose. "Scared I'd be forgotten like my mom was forgotten after the trees took her. I told Dad I was scared. He reminded me that my Noble name was carved in stone. In the lighthouse. And that was the only place I still had a connection. It was mine."

"You didn't think you could stay with your dad?"

The confusion in Mason's eyes was heartbreaking as he slowly shook his head.

"Dad can't afford a home for me. He only has an apartment, after he sold our house. There are no trees at his apartment." He shrugged. "Dad always said I only had a home because of Ma, and after Ma left, I didn't have a home no more."

Who says that to their child? Rebecca wanted to find Dennis Alton and toss him in the ocean herself.

"Speaking of Ma, were you able to find out if that body was hers? Some lady came and rubbed the inside of my cheek with a stick, so I'm assuming that was to match our DNA."

"That's right. It's how they take DNA samples, and we don't have the results yet. I'm sorry to say we don't know much more now than we did when I last saw you." Rebecca glanced at Benji. "Mason, how did you get the gun?"

Mason hung his head and shook it from side to side. What with his having been so eager to tell his story, Rebecca pondered his reluctance to answer. Was he protecting someone?

"Mason, I'm really curious. You see, I'm sure you know

from all the crime shows you watch that people in your... situation can't buy a gun legally. Did a friend give it to you? Did you feel the need to protect yourself?"

The man-child mumbled something she couldn't decipher.

"What was that? Can you say it louder, please?"

"I don't want anyone to get in trouble."

"That's very admirable of you. Who would get in trouble if you told me that?"

"Do I have to say?"

"Your whole life, you've felt like no one believed you. I'm sitting here, along with my friend, Benji, and all we want to do is believe you. Just tell us the truth, because I will believe you."

Mason lifted his chin and looked at Rebecca. "You did say you believed me back there." He forced a heavy sigh through his lips. "It was my dad."

"Your dad gave you the gun? Did he give you the bullets too?"

"Yeah. He even gave me extra. He didn't do anything wrong, though. He said that I'd need it to protect my leg-a-see and the lighthouse. He was only trying to help. It's the nicest thing he's done for me in a long time."

Rebecca released a long breath. "I have some other bad news for you."

"What's that?" His eyes made him look like an abused puppy waiting to be kicked.

"Your father has gone missing."

"Are you going to bring the dogs back to find him?"

"We're hoping it won't come to that, but we might. His car is still where he went missing. Do you know of any place in town he might go? Does he have a place that's important to him? Any friends still on the island?"

Mason shook his head. "He never cared about the house,

and I don't know many other places in town except the park and the church. And the beaches. But he never cared about the beaches. He hated the water and never learned how to swim."

That was an interesting bit of information. And even more proof that his suicide note about going to swim into the ocean was a complete forgery.

She didn't know if it was sleep deprivation talking, but the idea of tossing Alton into the ocean immediately got more appealing.

Mason rubbed his ears. "Maybe he went to see Jeff."

"Jeff?" Rebecca clenched her hands together to try to stay calm. "Do you know Jeff's last name?"

He shook his head. "He's Dad's friend. He was at Dad's when I went to see him. He was the one who told Dad about the lighthouse being torn down and the meeting that would decide if it happened. I asked him what he meant, and he said if someone didn't step in and bring people's attention to it, the lighthouse would be destroyed forever."

"Can you tell me how your dad knows Jeff?"

Mason lifted a shoulder. "Dad said they've been friends for a long time now. Years, since before Ma was taken by the trees."

"What does Jeff look like?"

"Um, Italian, with the slicked hair. Sort of like a bad guy from the movies. No offense to him."

Rebecca's pulse picked up speed. "Had you met Jeff before?"

"You know, I forgot, but when he introduced us, Dad said, 'you remember Jeff.' And I had met him a long time ago before the hospital. Maybe once or twice." Mason rubbed his ears harder. "Something must've been wrong with his car."

"What? Are you remembering something from the past?"

"He showed up late, after the game that night. He and Dad

went outside to talk. Then when he left, he drove Ma's car. His didn't work or something."

"Was that before or after your mom was taken by the trees?"

"After. Because he missed the whole game. He missed seeing Ma. They had me go to bed, but you know, I didn't do that. And I remember him telling Dad it would be okay, but they had to hurry before the sun came up." Mason's face went ghost white.

Rebecca watched as the dots connected in his mind.

"Wait. They had to hurry. Does that mean that my dad hurt my mom, and Jeff helped him hide her body in the trees?"

"I'm not sure, Mason, but I'm going to go ask him about it. I'm sorry to do this, but I have to step out for a moment, and that means I have to handcuff you again. Okay?"

He weakly nodded as he compliantly extended one hand.

After cuffing Mason to the table, Rebecca glanced over at Benji. "Want to come with me?"

Mason slumped onto the table and rested his head on his restrained arm, the notion of his father killing his mother becoming all-consuming.

Benji gave her a sad shake of his head and indicated that she should follow him.

After they were outside the interrogation room and it had been relocked, she glanced around the halls, noting that Dr. Montgomery had taken a seat at the only unused desk in the bullpen.

Benji faced Rebecca, looking like someone had kicked his puppy. "I've got to leave. Got called to a new case."

For a second, Rebecca thought she might cry. She blinked, refusing to let a single tear show itself. "So soon?"

She knew the answer before she'd asked. He had to go whenever he was called.

"Yeah. Sucks, but you know how it is."

Yes, she did.

Forcing a bright smile, she made her voice as cheerful as she could. "Well, next time you're in my neck of the woods, stop by. Maybe we'll make it to the beach."

He pulled her into a hug. "I will. Now go get your bad guy."

She squeezed him tight and stepped away. "You get yours too."

With a little salute, Benji walked away. She watched him go.

Once, he'd been her favorite person. The person she trusted most.

Now?

She turned her back on her past and returned to the present as she spoke into her radio. "Hey, Locke, I need you to keep an eye on Mason here at the station. I've got to see a man about his travel plans."

42

Mason's words echoed in Rebecca's mind despite how horribly tired she was. Had Jeff Benton helped Dennis Alton bury Maria's body? Her mind raced, trying to arrange the pieces into a complete picture.

Alton was at the lighthouse for much of the ordeal, but he did disappear before many of the others. How long ago was that? Eighteen hours? If Benton was involved in Alton's disappearance, he's had all night to hide the body. But where would he go? Does he even know the island—

"Where would he go?" Rebecca bounced the thought off her deputy as he stepped out of his Explorer and opened the door to hers, having just returned from the Tidepool Motel.

Darian got into the driver's seat. "He doesn't live on the island, so we can mark off all the hidden places and focus on what he would know."

"The lighthouse, the town hall, the old Alton Place."

"I'm betting he's not trying to dump a body at the town hall. The Alton Place is on the way to the lighthouse."

"And there're holes and piles of dirt to hide a body. A construction site."

"It's perfect." Darian put the Explorer in reverse and got them on the road before Rebecca could put her seat belt on.

"If our instincts are wrong, we're going to feel pretty silly tomorrow when Richmond Vale calls to complain about a corpse on the lawn."

Darian laughed at her lame joke. "True. Besides, he has an entire ocean at his disposal. It's one of the best ways to dump a body."

It was Rebecca's turn to laugh. "It is? Have you already forgotten that we had two corpses wash up only a couple days ago?"

"Nope, but if he chops the body up…" Darian grimaced. "Fish food."

"Of course, if our instincts are right, the cadaver dogs are going to find Paddy's and J.J.'s bodies buried under those fancy condos that Coastal Properties built, since Viviane let us know that Jeff's company bought both properties."

The spurt of adrenaline Rebecca had felt at putting the whole picture together started to fade. Taking several deep breaths, she tried to clear her thinking.

"Let's hit the Alton Place, then."

Darian nodded and the cruiser sped up. "He's a fool, if so. Cadaver dogs can find a corpse even if it's been buried in concrete. I bet he doesn't know that."

"Maybe he thinks we already used the dogs, and we won't bring them back. Since we're still missing two other people. At least. I'll have to remember to call Lettinger and tell her to get the dogs to check where Paddy's Pub was as well as J.J. Gossard's old homesite."

"He's a serial killer?"

"He's a greedy bastard who'll kill to score a property. And sounds like Dennis Alton is too. Or was. But honestly, we won't know until we get him in and start asking questions." She glanced over at her deputy. "Labels don't matter tonight.

He's a killer with no compunction. Most likely he killed Alton, his partner, to eliminate the possibility that he'd go down with a confession after we found Maria's body."

"Roger that." Darian slowed as they got close to their destination. "How are we going to make contact when we do find him?"

Rebecca thought it through. "Let me take the lead. We've already spoken once, at least. And he thinks he has me fooled. He likes to play the chameleon, mimicking the person he's trying to win over to get them to trust him."

"He's here." Darian slowed even more as they saw a car parked on the gravel lane that ran between the beginnings of houses. The same car Jeff Benton had driven Richmond Vale to the lighthouse in. The trunk was open, but it looked like the light inside wasn't working. Only the glow of moonlight lit up the jumbled array of construction.

"That's definitely Benton's vehicle." Rebecca knew it could be Dennis Alton out here instead if he'd faked his own death. Stolen Jeff's car after dispatching his partner. They'd know soon enough. They both released their seat belts, ready to jump out.

The cruiser pulled in behind the car. Darian verified the dashcam was recording as the dust faded. Gravel hadn't been poured this far back, so the road was only packed earth. "We gonna get those body cams anytime soon?"

"I'm working on it."

"Would be nice to have for situations like this." His head was constantly moving as he looked for Jeff Benton.

"What I have in mind requires a few additional steps." Rebecca spotted movement near one of the construction trucks parked just a few yards away. Benton appeared from around the rear of the truck and opened the vehicle's driver door. "There he is."

She opened the cruiser door and stepped out, keeping her

body behind the door. Pulling out her flashlight, she pointed the beam in his direction. "Jeff Benton."

"That's me. Didn't mean to worry anyone." He pulled off a set of heavy leather gloves covered in gray and tossed them into the cab.

"Kind of late for you to be out here working, isn't it?" Rebecca lifted her flashlight and pointed it directly at his face, blinding him so he couldn't see her movements.

He laughed as he held his hand up in front of his eyes. "Not late, Sheriff. Early. You chased the crew off yesterday and this needs to be finished. The rest of the guys will be here when the sun rises in a few hours, but I thought I'd go ahead and get this last bit of yesterday's pour finished so we can get back on schedule. Soon as it's done, I'm moving on to other projects."

I bet you are.

Did this man really think she was stupid enough to believe that bullshit story? If he was indeed pouring concrete, it wasn't for a house.

It was for a grave.

With the two of them blocking Jeff's ability to get to his car, she could only hope the crew for this job site was a paranoid group. It was relatively common for workers to leave the keys inside the truck so the vehicle or machine could be used as soon as the crew arrived in the morning.

Darian moved up the left side of the Explorer, almost level with her as she moved forward to stand behind the parked car. "What are you working on?"

"Finishing up a garage foundation. Was I being too loud? Did someone complain? The cement mixer can be a bit noisy."

Benton's trunk was empty. Two deep, thin tire lines tracked through the dirt leading past where he was standing.

The missing luggage. He hauled Dennis Alton out in his luggage? How did he get a man that tall into a case that small? Shit.

Rebecca unsnapped her holster as Darian did the same. Benton didn't seem to have a weapon on him, but until he was patted down, they couldn't be sure.

"Yeah," she lied. "We got a call about some strange sounds coming from here. After all the mess with the lighthouse yesterday, we wanted to make sure no one was out here vandalizing the place." She forced a laugh. "You know how people get around construction sites. They always wanna play with the toys. Especially when they're drunk. Can you show us what you're working on?"

Benton laughed and turned to point behind him. "Well, it's not like I'm going to tear up my own company's project, now, am I?"

As she kept Benton distracted, Darian covered more ground. He was near the truck. His angle was bad, though. He'd have to expose himself to get to Benton while their suspect had a thick metal door to hide behind.

"Maybe not. But we still need to check it out. You're out here working without a light. That seems pretty strange, doesn't it? I'd hate for your company to sue me later because we walked out here and didn't bother to actually take a look around."

"Of course. Come on back." He turned as if to head back the way he'd come.

"Sir, I'm going to have to ask you to stop right there."

The smile didn't falter. "Is there a problem, Sheriff?"

"Just stay in the light, Mr. Benton."

"And raise your hands."

With his smarmy smile in place, Benton raised his hands to shoulder height. A second later, he dove into the dormant construction truck, swinging the door closed before Darian could reach it.

Shit.

Rebecca drew her Armory 1911, pointing the barrel at the windshield just as Benton turned on the brights, blinding her. The engine roared to life. Gravel flew as he hit the gas, heading right toward her.

Bam. Bam. Bam.

Her bullets punched the glass, but the truck didn't slow. Rebecca barely jumped to safety as the truck bolted past her and down the unfinished road.

43

Rebecca was already at a full run before she heard Darian curse and take off as well. Having been closer to the cruiser, she reached the driver's door before him. In *The Dukes of Hazzard* style, Darian slid across the hood and landed on the passenger side, diving into the open door.

"Go! Go, go, go!" He held onto the side of his seat and pulled the door closed as she spun the cruiser around and took off after the truck.

The screech of tires on pavement echoed in the night, letting her know Benton had reached the road already. Rebecca took the turn fast, sliding the back end on the gravel. She slammed on the gas, pulling the Explorer straight as she shot after him.

"Hit the lights." Both her hands were wrapped so tight on the steering wheel to keep the vehicle under control that she couldn't reach the switch herself. Benton's taillights glowed just ahead of them. They were catching up quick.

Darian pulled his seat belt around with one hand before turning on the lights and siren with the other. Once he was belted in, he grabbed the radio. "The staties might still be in the area. I'll have them block off the bridge, if nothing else."

Rebecca nodded and listened as he called it in.

Now that she was heading straight on a road, she got to belt herself in as well. "He's not getting away. Let dispatch know we've got a possible body dump as well. We'll need the techs back."

The lights ahead of them flicked off.

She growled low in her throat. "Dammit! This idiot turned off his lights to try and hide."

"Shit! He's going to kill someone."

She tried to picture a map of the area. "This is a straight stretch. I'm going to try to PIT him." She didn't see any other alternative. Every moment they were on the road like this put more people in danger. There weren't many houses around, but they'd soon be reaching the main roads that led from the beaches to the mainland, where tourists would be.

Darian straightened himself in his seat so he could brace his feet. "Go for it."

Blowing out a breath, she applied more pressure to the accelerator again. The tires went onto the shoulder as she lined her bumper up with the back passenger's side panel. Darian braced his arms. This was the safest thing they could do, but it was by no means safe.

And she wasn't about to tell him that this was the first time she'd tried this outside of the training track.

With a controlled twist of the wheel, she slammed her Explorer into the truck's back end and pushed it around. His lightweight bed swung wildly away, crossing over the line, and she eased off the gas a hair. Adrenaline pounded through her veins, and it felt like everything was happening in slow motion.

If he got control of the truck, she was still close enough to hit him again. The whole point of this maneuver was to spin the fleeing vehicle out of control so it would be safely pushed off the road.

The truck went off the right side of the road, bouncing over the ruts and dips, then veered hard to the left.

Darian grunted, his arms still locking him in place. "He's making a break for the bridge."

Considering they were practically on the southernmost tip of the island, that meant he'd plow through the more populated areas of town. Thank goodness it was the middle of the night. Not that time of day mattered that much at a vacation destination.

"Dammit."

Rebecca chose not to go after him. Instead, she stayed on the road and hit the gas again. Even going slower, Benton was cutting straight through a marshy area while she followed the road around.

"There he is." Darian pointed. "He's coming back to pavement."

Not if she could help it.

Rebecca waited until the truck skittered back onto the road. The oversized vehicle wasn't completely under control and swayed back and forth. She watched the swaying movements and timed it just right.

"Hold on."

She slammed her foot down on the gas, reminding herself not to lock her arms. The cruiser jumped forward as the truck bed swung to her left. The reinforced grill smashed into the lower side of the bed behind the back tire. This time, she didn't let up on the gas as she turned to the left. The momentum of her heavy vehicle slammed into the truck and forced it around, then over to the far side of the road.

Benton's front end followed. The soft, sandy shoulder

caught his front tire. The front half of the truck started to dip, and Rebecca slammed on the brakes. Shrieks of metal on metal rang out, and she spun to the left. This was precisely what cruisers were built for, and they jerked to a stop as the truck flipped over.

Instinctively, she flinched, closing her eyes as a tire whizzed over the hood of their cruiser. The crunch and crash of the wreck could be heard easily over the scream of the siren as the truck continued to roll. The road dipped down slightly before a small clearing.

She opened her eyes and watched the truck roll a few more turns, slamming into the bald cypress trees the Noble family had planted generations ago. She and Darian were out of the cruiser an instant later. Darian's gun was already up and pointed.

The wrecked vehicle had landed on the passenger side, the undercarriage resting against a tree, a few broken tree limbs scattered on top and all around it. Rebecca stepped around the door, taking it all in around the sights on the barrel of her weapon.

A loud crack of glass shot out.

"He's got a gun. He's using the butt of a rifle to smash out the windshield." Darian's voice was barely above a whisper as he shuffled forward and down the embankment. "Drop the weapon, Jeff Benton!"

There was no backing down now.

"No one else has to die, Jeff. Drop the weapon and come out with your hands up."

There was another crack, and this time, Rebecca was positioned where she could see the heavy wooden stock slam into the spiderwebbed safety glass, bowing it out from its frame.

"If Mason had done his job right and offed all those people in the lighthouse like we told him to, none of the rest of this would've had to happen." Benton continued to hammer away. "It was a simple task and the idiot screwed it up. I'm not afraid of you, you know. You couldn't even take out a crazy kid who'd shot a little old lady!"

Rebecca understood now.

Suicide by cop. That was what the plan had been all along. Not for themselves. But it was what Alton and Benton had planned for Mason. A bloody shootout in a giant stone fortress that would have ended in several dead, including the shooter. Neither of them had planned on her team taking the time to talk to Mason and believe his ramblings enough to investigate anything.

And once the shootout happened, no one would want to look at a landmark where so many of their neighbors had died. Selling it would've been easy after that. And Benton would've made a hefty commission from the development. Alton too. Money they'd split.

"Dennis sold out his wife and son to you. So why did you kill him?"

"He wasn't supposed to kill his wife. All he had to do was talk her into selling. But he couldn't hold his temper."

Rebecca saw the writing on the wall. "And calling you made you complicit, right?"

"Damn straight." He replaced the rifle with his foot and began to kick at the fractured glass.

She couldn't see the rifle now. Not good. She needed to keep him talking. "What happened?"

"That's when he told me about her will. How the land didn't belong to him even after she was dead, and we'd have to wait seven years and get his kid committed too. The sale of the Alton property was supposed to be our one and only transaction, but he wanted more. And he didn't want to wait for his payday either."

"So he blackmailed you into hiring him."

Part of Rebecca hoped that Dennis Alton wasn't truly dead, so she could toss him in jail until he rotted. It wasn't likely, considering it looked like he'd been transported in a small suitcase back to his old property.

"And then what does he do? After all this time, multiple million-dollar deals under his belt, he goes off and gets himself caught! I told him to move her body and dump it somewhere it couldn't be found once the heat was off. But he got lazy, left it, and you guys finally connected the dots. I couldn't let him turn on me. I didn't kill Maria. That was all him."

The hole in the windshield was finally big enough for Benton to crawl out.

"Put the gun down!" Darian barked as the flash of metal glinted in the spinning red-and-blue lights. He was angling to the right, trying for a better shot and the barrel turned, following his movements.

"You're not going to—"

Rebecca didn't wait. As soon as Benton's hand came into view on the forestock of the rifle—the only part of him she could see from where she was standing—she squeezed the trigger.

Benton screamed and the rifle fell.

Darian fired right after her, already running forward. His aim was dead-on, though, and Benton screamed again.

She reached the wreck moments after Darian. He slammed his foot down on the rifle, pulling the laminated glass down with it and exposing a bleeding Jeff Benton crouched down, clutching his left hand with his right. One shot had taken him in the forearm, while the other had gone through his hand. Rebecca briefly wondered which of them had been the better shot.

Benton wasn't going to be picking up his rifle, or anything else, for a while.

"Okay, let's try this again." Rebecca darted around Darian, grabbing Benton's collar and dragging him across the shattered windshield into the grass and onto his stomach. "Jeff Benton, you're under arrest."

44

Rebecca held up her badge at the doors of the Saint Brides Correctional Mental Health Ward in Coastal Ridge. After inspecting it closely, a guard ushered her inside.

She'd spent the majority of her mandatory desk duty sleeping and dealing with paperwork. Desk duty after firing her gun was a requirement 'til she was cleared. Part of her wished she'd done more than just wound Benton, since it was already time for her to go back to full duty.

Darian had been under the same restriction, so Hoyt had dealt with transferring the prisoners. This would be her first time seeing Mason since she'd let him know about Jeff Benton's confession and the fate of his dad.

He'd had a breakdown after that and been transferred here in an ambulance after being sedated by Dr. Montgomery. The woman hadn't left his side the entire time. She seemed to feel that she'd failed him before and was now hell-bent on correcting that.

It had worked. A judge had agreed to move him to this medium-security prison with a strong focus on substance abuse and mental health. That made Rebecca feel a bit better.

Plus, according to Montgomery, it was a temporary stop for Mason until he eventually found a more permanent placement.

The guard escorted Rebecca down the hall and into a small visitation room with wire mesh-embedded glass windows the guards in the hall could watch through. Mason Alton was seated at a metal table, and he smiled as she was let in.

"I'll be right outside. Hit the button if you need anything."

Rebecca nodded and the guard shut the door, locking her in. "How are you doing, Mason?"

"Much better now. Thank you. Dr. Montgomery said I'm making progress. I'm not seeing the past so much now. That helps a lot."

She smiled. "I'm glad."

"How's Nora doing? And the other people from that group? Did you tell them I said I was sorry? And Nora's son?"

"I did tell them. Nora said she understands. She loves the lighthouse as much as you do and admits she might've gone to great lengths, as you did, to save it in her younger days."

Rebecca wasn't going to tell Mason that Chad said to tell him to go screw himself and hoped he burned in Hell for eternity. Mason didn't need to hear that, and it wouldn't help anyone.

"She's a very nice lady. I feel terrible about what I did to her."

"Nora's arm is in a sling, but that isn't slowing her down. The lighthouse, by the way, is not being sold."

Mason's head lifted, and he smiled. "That's good to know. But it's not because of me. I know that now. It's because of Nora and her friends. And I almost screwed it all up. I'm glad the lighthouse has someone like her to keep it safe."

Rebecca leaned in and whispered conspiratorially, "You wanna hear something really amazing?"

He nodded with a grin.

"The trees your family planted, the ones that stopped Jeff from getting away, they're going to be used to rebuild the interior of the lighthouse. It turns out, your family had always planned for that. After your grandmother told us about them, Nora looked into it. Bald cypress wood was originally used on the stairway and interior structure. And since the source of the wood was right there, and sustainable, they'll be harvesting the trees for the wood, making it much cheaper and easier to restore the building."

He beamed at her. "I knew the trees were important. Ma always told me that. I just...I couldn't remember why. My head was all messed up. I'm glad Nora figured it out. I guess she's busy working on all that now?"

Rebecca grinned. "You bet she is. And she's been cracking the whip because there's this new Lovecraft Symposium coming to town, and she wants the lighthouse open for them."

Mason frowned and shook his head. "What's a Lovecraft?"

"H.P. Lovecraft. He was an author who wrote a strange new genre of horror." She scanned her memory for the tiniest nugget to share and could only think of one thing. "I know very little about Lovecraft, but I remember hearing something about an ancient god that lived under the ocean and was so horrible that people would be driven mad from just seeing him or hearing him speak."

Rebecca winced, wondering if she'd hit a little too close to home. *Good job. Let the one thing you know about Lovecraft be that.*

He grew thoughtful, though, not afraid or sad. After several moments, he met her gaze. "I wonder if that's what happened to me. I got too close to the ocean and bam! Crazy Mason."

Maybe she shouldn't have, but Rebecca laughed. A second later, he did too.

It was nice to see. This man in front of her was remarkably different from the one she'd met at the lighthouse.

She grinned. "Hmm. Just in case, maybe you should stay away from reading Lovecraft."

He shrugged. "I'm pretty sure they don't have anything like that in the library at Golden Acres anyway."

"Is that where you'll be going? Back to Golden Acres in Norfolk?"

"Dr. Montgomery thinks so. I'd like that. It means Gramma can come see me there. Dad can't stop her now. I didn't know he had been." His eyes filled with tears. "It's good to know not everyone hates me, even if I deserve it."

Rebecca reached across the table and squeezed Mason's hand. "I don't hate you. Neither does Nora or Gracie or Bob or Chuck. All my deputies like you too. You're not a bad person, Mason, just because you did a bad thing."

He wiped his face with his sleeve. "I won't do bad things anymore."

"I know you won't. You doing okay? Have you decided what you want us to do with your father's ashes?"

Mason's nostrils flared. "Flush them down the toilet. I don't care."

Rebecca had already explained everything she'd learned about that night. Poor kid. It'd been hard to go over all those terrible details, but she could tell it was better for him to know than wonder.

He looked at her, something he seemed to do more often. Looking people in the eye was hard for him, and he usually stared at the table or the wall instead. "What about Paddy Pearce and J.J. Gossard? Did you find their bodies?"

"Not yet. But we've reopened the cases now that we know about Jeff Benton. He approached both of them in an effort to buy their land. When they wouldn't sell, they went missing."

"Are you going to call in the dogs again?"

"Yep. I'm sure they'll find them."

She didn't tell Mason that the bodies were most likely hidden in the concrete used during construction. Which was what Jeff Benton had tried to do to Dennis Alton after killing him and stuffing him into a large rolling suitcase. As badly as he'd taken the news of his father's death, he didn't need to know the gruesome details.

"It was because of what you told us that we were able to link all their deaths together."

Mason's chin dipped again. "I wish I'd spoken up sooner. Or that the other sheriff had believed me. Maybe then, J.J. and Paddy wouldn't have had to die."

Rebecca had nothing to say to that. He was right. If Wallace had listened to young Mason and not written him off as a non-credible witness, things might've been completely different.

"I'm tired now."

His face was drawn and pale. It was like each word he'd spoken had taken a piece of his health.

"I'll let you go rest then, but Mason," she waited until his tired, sad eyes met hers, "none of that was your fault. Police are people too. And sometimes, we make mistakes. That's not your fault. You did your best. And you were just a child."

His lips tipped up at the corners a little bit. "I'll try to remember that."

With nothing else to say, she got up and pressed the button. The door opened.

She glanced back to the man-child sitting at the table, his head on his folded hands. "He's tired."

The guard nodded. "I'll get his nurses. We'll take care of him. Don't worry."

Rebecca thanked him and allowed herself to be led out. There was no way she wouldn't worry about Mason. She made a promise to herself that she'd keep checking in on him.

Her mind immediately jumped to Robert Leigh. Two men driven insane by the horror of what had happened to them on the island.

Mason might be able to do some healing with the right help. Benji had notified Rebecca that Mason's original doctor, Dinton, had been dismissed from the institution for, among other violations, taking money under the table. And Dennis Alton had been one of the people paying him.

As she stepped out the front door and into the watery sunlight of a stormy morning, her phone rang. It was Viviane.

"Please tell me that everything is peaches and cream on the island."

Viviane didn't laugh. "I wish I could. You're going to need to drive back as soon as you can."

Rebecca sighed and headed to her cruiser. The front was all scratched up from ramming the truck, but it still ran like a champ.

"What's happened?"

She really didn't want to know.

"We've got two dead bodies inside the Old Witch's Cottage. And from what I heard, it looks like a scene from a horror movie."

The End
To be continued...

Thank you for reading.
All of the *Shadow Island Series* books can be found on Amazon.

ACKNOWLEDGMENTS

How does one properly thank everyone involved in taking a dream and making it a reality? Here goes.

In addition to our families, whose unending support provided the foundation for us to find the time and energy to put these thoughts on paper, we want to thank the editors who polished our words and made them shine.

Many thanks to our publisher for risking taking on two newbies and giving us the confidence to become bona fide authors.

More than anyone, we want to thank you, our readers, for sharing your most important asset, your time, with this book. We hope with all our hearts we made it worthwhile.

Much love,

Mary & Lori

ABOUT THE AUTHOR

Mary Stone

Mary Stone lives among the majestic Blue Ridge Mountains of East Tennessee with her two dogs, four cats, a couple of energetic boys, and a very patient husband.

As a young girl, she would go to bed every night, wondering what type of creature might be lurking underneath. It wasn't until she was older that she learned that the creatures she needed to most fear were human.

Today, she creates vivid stories with courageous, strong heroines and dastardly villains. She invites you to enter her world of serial killers, FBI agents but never damsels in distress. Her female characters can handle themselves, going toe-to-toe with any male character, protagonist or antagonist.

Discover more about Mary Stone on her website.
www.authormarystone.com

Lori Rhodes

As a tiny girl, from the moment Lori Rhodes first dipped her toe into the surf on a barrier island of Virginia, she was in love. When she grew up and learned all the deep, dark secrets and horrible acts people could commit against each other, she couldn't stop the stories from coming out of the other end of her pen. Somehow, her magical island and the darkness got mixed together and ended up in her first novel. Now, she spends her days making sure the guests at her beach rental cottages are happy, and her nights dreaming up the characters who love her island as much as she does.

Connect with Mary Online

- facebook.com/authormarystone
- twitter.com/MaryStoneAuthor
- goodreads.com/AuthorMaryStone
- bookbub.com/profile/3378576590
- pinterest.com/MaryStoneAuthor
- instagram.com/marystoneauthor
- tiktok.com/@authormarystone

Made in the USA
Coppell, TX
20 May 2023